EXHALE

Q. Imagine

To Susan,

Don't give up on your dreams
Enjoy the journey!

- Q

Copyright © 2020 Qiana Marks

All rights reserved

The characters and events portrayed in this book are fictitious. Any similarity to real persons, living or dead, is coincidental and not intended by the author.

No part of this book may be reproduced, or stored in a retrieval system, or transmitted in any form or by any means, electronic, mechanical, photocopying, recording, or otherwise, without express written permission of the publisher.

ISBN-13: 9798645518400
ISBN-10: 1477123456

Cover design by: Alonzo Boone
Library of Congress Control Number: PAu 3-943-618
Printed in the United States of America

*To you, for sharing these moments with a part of me.
To my family and friends that have kept me strong
and to my own Alice, for telling me to keep going.
Thank you.*

"Let love guide you, not fear."

RALPH SMART

CONTENTS

Title Page
Copyright
Dedication
Epigraph
Introduction
Preface
Exhale

DAY 1	1
Day 2	18
DAY 3	34
Day 4	72
Day 5	81
Chapter I	104
Chapter II	117
Chapter III	131
Chapter IV	139
Chapter V	148
Chapter VI	168
Chapter VII	180
Chapter VIII	198

Chapter IX	215
Chapter X	220
Chapter XI	224
Chapter XII	238
About The Author	249
Books In This Series	251

INTRODUCTION

It is said in anxious moments, people are prone to hold in their breath. To hold in and bottle the stress when sometimes you need to Exhale.

PREFACE

I remember the naive girl that started this novel, without any idea on what a journey this experience would be. As I found myself within these pages and within the story of Jane Mackenzie. I found out who I was when no one was looking. My true essence. Since we grow up in a world that tests our imperfections, shames our mistakes in hopes of rewarding our triumphs. Though looking back, I cherish the naive little girl who dreamt of beauty and love. As I humbly cherish this journey that's led me to you, in Jane's exhale. A new breath of life.

EXHALE

DAY 1

As she walks down the cold concrete sidewalk, she can hear the pitter patter of her clogs hitting the ground.

Click. Clack

Click. Clack.

A melody to the day; A catchy tune to make this evening walk home a little more interesting.

Click. Clack

Click. Clack.

This steady beat becomes the rhythm to the symphony this city has to offer. The hustle and bustle of cars driving by become the brass instruments. As the chatter of the city dwellers on every corner become the sultry piano of the song. The brisk wind of autumn that blows the fallen leaves through the skyscrapers. They become the wind instruments of the song; the part you can't help but hum to.

The sounds of the city sings a beautiful tale about life and all of its endeavors, as Jane pays attention to the tune of the day and simply can't get it out of her head. A brief mixtape to her life, an interesting take out of an insignificant moment. And as she

Q. IMAGINE

dwells on the many spectacles around her, she can't help but notice the rhythm of New York City. How everything flows.

"I wonder if my presence right here adds to the rhythm of the day", she says. "Is this the place where I need to be. Right here and right now, in this very moment."

Her thoughts say 'duh' since it's the only place where she is. As she gazes at the many men and women along the sidewalk, either in their business suits or casual wear as they hold exhaustion upon their faces.

From the people walking in the same direction and those walking the opposite, she sees the many shades and sizes of everyone that makes her feel like a grain of sand. One spec in a sea of many, as the sun lowering in the sky starts to capture her attention. She realizes she may have spent too much time on her walk so she speeds up her pace. She hurries home as her long and curly brown hair sways with the wind.

But as her pace quickens and she gets into a rhythm with her speed walking, she slams into a man's shoulder. The collision knocks her off balance as she stumbles to the ground.

"Whoa! Excuse me!" Jane says, gathering her footing to angrily side-eye the rude man.

The fellow pedestrians blatantly walk around the two as the man who collided into Jane keeps walking, seemingly without an inkling in the sky. His disregard angers her, provoking Jane to give him a piece of her mind.

She yells out to him, "Excuse me! Watch where you're going!"

To her surprise, he turns around only to meet Jane's angry gaze. She hopes he gets the hint with the scowl on her face, even though her anger is slightly swayed with his handsome looks.

His all black attire compliments his suave, alluring appearance as his chiseled face and arms make his clothes look even better. He has deep, dark eyes that makes her skin crawl and hairs raise since he gazes into her eyes as if she is a vessel and not a human. She tries sizing him up but that only raises the tension as his gazes gets a little darker.

She mutters again, "Watch where you're going," as their eyes remain locked. Jane starts to feel her 5'6" slim yet curvy adolescent frame is no match against his 6-foot chiseled form and ominous approach. His eyes gaze down at her long, red and black checkerboard skirt as they begin to drift a little higher over her plain white blouse and black blazer.

"Why don't you take a picture?", Jane says, feeling creeped out with his silence.

He gives her another look up and down and says, "Guess no one taught you how to talk to people."

"Well maybe I'd be nicer if you would say excuse me, especially before pushing me out of your way."

He says, "You've got some attitude for a prep kid." He gazes at her school logo on the right side of her blazer.

"But what else can you expect from the world today. Maybe you should pay more attention to your surroundings. I mean, it is a city. A pretty rich kid should pay more attention and be more careful who you approach."

Jane playfully jumps back, pretending to be afraid of his warning. She laughs and says, "Or maybe you should watch where you're going or say excuse me, but I guess it would be too pain-

Q. IMAGINE

ful for you to give an apology. Classy guy like you should have better manners. But to quote you earlier...what else can you expect from the world these days."

She stares at him dauntingly before walking away. Though as she walks away, he says "I saw you, you just didn't see me."

"Maybe I wanted your attention", he says with a sly look on his face.

He takes one lasting gaze at her before he walks away but his eerie last words give Jane a distasteful feeling in her heart.

She loses sight of the stranger as a large crowd of people begin to walk in Jane's direction. She shakes off the creepy vibe he gives her and turns around to continue her walk back home.

"And I wanted to go to college in this place."

Upon approaching her block, she feels a sigh of relief as her feet begin to feel sore in her noisy clogs. She slows down her pace and takes in the few moments left of the evening before entering her house. She just wants to capture the sky. The beautiful portrait above her gives Jane a sensual feeling. She stops for a moment, gazing deeply into the pastel sky and forgetting the world around her until Jane hears a door open up a few feet away. She sees her small, petite mother peeping her head out of the door prompting Jane to yell down the block, "I'm coming. I know it's late." Her mother sees her standing there and starts to shake her head.

"You're late and I hope you see it's almost dark."

Jane mutters, "I know. I know. I'm coming."

She steps upon her stoop and hears the voices of her family inside of the house, with her keen sense of smell picking up the wispy smells of chopped garlic sizzling on the frying pan. She hears her mother singing to old classics jazz songs like Strange Fruit, chuckling at her mother's attempt to emulate the singer since they coincidentally have the same first name. The singing becomes overshadowed by the abrupt muffled sounds of an electric guitar. The noise stems from upstairs, prompting her to assume it's coming from her brother's room.

Jane is happy to hear that everyone is home as she looks forward to releasing the load of a heavy backpack. Though when she steps up on the stairs and prepares to walk inside the house, her acute ears tune into a whisper she hears from down the block.

"Jane" she hears echo as a shadow appears down the block. She lets curiosity keep her still as her hand is still placed on the nob of the front door. She's curious to see who it is, as the reoccurring call of her name flows through her mental encyclopedia of people she knows.

"What?" she whispers, still tempted to walk through the door. As the stranger approaches and continues to call out her name as well as ignoring her response.

"Who is it?" she asks. The anticipation grips her heart but out from afar, the shadow is illuminated as the image of a teenage boy. He walks closer and sees that it's her friend.

Jane puts her hand on her hip, annoyed and says "Tola, today is not the day to be creepy."

"Who said I was trying to be creepy?" he humbly responds.

"I did. You were the one calling out my name. In the dark. In Brooklyn."

The young man comes closer, revealing his long, curly blonde hair in the luminesce of the streetlight. His emerald green eyes start to shimmer as a smile perks on his face and hers as well.

"I was trying to keep a low profile. I know your parents are home and I didn't want them to hear me."

Jane takes a deep breath as she walks off of her stoop to talk to him.

He says, "Why are you so on edge?" As he greets her with a smile and opens his arms to give her a big hug.

"Some creep pissed me off earlier." Jane says. "He nearly tried to take my shoulder off as I was walking home."

"Yea, it's always crazy during rush hour." Tola says.

"Ugh, tell me about it!"

Jane and Tola stay embraced as they both wait for the moment to let go of each other. They let go and simply look at each other and laugh, breaking the awkward tension of the moment. Jane looks at him and says, "So what do I owe this nightly encounter?"

He says, "I wanted to share something with you tonight, something special."

Jane says, "Like what?"

Tola gives her a sly look as he proceeds to not respond.

Jane sighs and says, "Just spare me the shenanigans tonight. Every night with you somehow turns into something. Last time you said there was mischief in the air and we almost got arrested. And I had to lie to my parents about where I was. It's already been an eventful night, I think..."

He says, "C'mon Jane, don't be like that. Tonight, is a completely different night and that happened once."

He gives her a cute smile in an attempt to sway her opinion. She admires his attempt and gives him a smile with sarcasm. She says, "I'm sorry but whatever my mom is making inside has my name on it. I don't think my stomach would want to miss out on it, no offense."

Trying to keep her interest, he pleads, "C'mon Jane. Don't think about your stomach. What happened to your mantras on living in the present? Never taking a moment for granted or whatever. The food will always be here but I won't. This will be worth your while."

Jane looks back at her home and looks back at him, unsure if she should just let him down and listen to her stomach. She sways as she contemplates but begins to gain interest.

She says, "First, tell me what we're doing and you might strike some luck tonight."

Tola smiles as he puts his arm around her and says, "You know I wouldn't go this hard if I knew you wouldn't like it. But yea, let's take a stroll. It's a quick stroll. Nothing big. Nothing too much."

Jane suddenly stops in her tracks and says, "Wait. Wait. Wait. I am not missing dinner just for a walk."

Jane walks away from Tola towards her house but Tola reaches out to grab her hand.

He says, "You're not missing dinner at all. We're just walking around the block. Nothing big, it'll be quick. I promise you'll like it."

And after seeing his reluctance to give up, Jane agrees but remembers her mother's expectation.

She says, "O.K. but I need to say something to my mom and put my stuff down. Give me a few minutes."

Tola agrees as he takes a seat on her stoop, flipping his black hood over his head as he rests his head on the railing. Jane walks in and throws her bag on the ground near the coat hanger, feeling relieved to finally stop lugging it all around. She walks into the kitchen, gives her mother a hug before interrupting her singing to ask her if she could step out before dinner.

"Hey Mom?"

Billie smiles at her, continuing to sing.

"Okay mom, I'm just going to step out for a few minutes. See you later."

Billie clears her throat as she points to the clock above the sink.

"You see what time it is, right?" Billie says.

"Yes, I know, but I haven't seen this friend in a while."

"Who is it?" Billie asks.

Jane hesitates, "Tola."

Billie sighs and says, "Make it quick. You know I don't like you hanging out with that older boy."

Jane says, "He's not that much older. And he graduated. That's a step-in life."

Billie turns her face up and says, "Jane, you need to be home before the table is set."

To which Jane replies, "I will. It won't be long. I already told him I can't miss dinner."

"Good."

Billie finally gives her consent as Jane quickly runs back towards the door in order to meet Tola outside. She grabs her keys with her wallet attached as she walks out of the door.

Stepping out of the house, Jane says, "Okay we need to make this quick. Mom was pretty adamant about me being home before the table is set."

Tola says, "Okay we'll just walk around the block."

    A smile shines on his face, only prompting Jane to smile. The two begin to walk down the block as they distance themselves further from Jane's house. She watches Tola as he pulls out a cannon and lights it. Jane is surprised by the exceedingly, large joint in his hand, as she laughs with no regret in her eyes.

She says, "Of course this would be the importance of this walk."

Tola jokingly shrugs his shoulders and says, "Yea. You know, business."

"And right before dinner? Wonderful. Tola you truly have some timing."

Q. IMAGINE

He takes two hits and passes it to her, as she surveys the joint before hitting it.

"What's in this?" she asks.

"This is premo stuff, Jane. I haven't even made much of a profit off of it because I keep smoking all of it."

When she takes a hit, she feels the burning sensation of the smoke flow from her mouth, filling up her lungs and her throat before exhaling slowly.

Jane looks at her friend as she nods her head in agreement. Jane says, "Wow, this stuff is premiere." before taking a few more pulls and feeling like she's walking on air.

Then the two silently walk along the sidewalk, taking a few more hits until they come back onto Jane's block. The conversation fades as they continue to walk in unison.

Jane jumps to the question "So how much do you have left?"

He says to her slowly as he's still recovering from the daze of the high.

"A good amount."

Jane smiles at Tola, batting her eyelashes. As he feels the spirit of the night and loving Jane's company, he gives in and says, "Alright but only because we're cool."

Jane smiles with success as they make the exchange. They walk up to Jane's door and Tola stops her from walking in. He says with his blood shot eyes, "I really do appreciate you, Jane."

"Why?" She asks.

"Because you're real."

"You don't hide your feelings and I respect you for that."

Jane smiles and says, "Well I really appreciate that. You're one of the very few people who appreciates that quality about me."

She quips before she walks through her door, "But don't get too soft on me."

"You're pretty awesome too. Thanks again for the night."

Tola says, "Yea, I'd hope you enjoy our time together. We don't spend as much time together as I liked to, since you're so busy getting ready for college and finishing up your last year."

She says, "Yea, not everyone can make a profit off of what you do. School is my gateway to journalism, saving the world through informative reports and catchy topics."

Tola laughs and says, "Yea I see your point. But still, you're seventeen and when you get the chance, hit me up if you want to hang out or if you need something. There's no need to be a stranger all of the time."

Tola backs away from the door, Jane smiles with her hand on the doorknob.

She says "Maybe I like my alone time. I get more work done."

He walks away and says, "Ahh well I know you'll hit me up for one thing. See ya later stranger."

"Bye Tola."

As soon as she steps through the front door, she grabs her bag and walks up the mahogany stained staircase towards her room. She glances at her mom who eyes her as she begins to seep up the table, briefly overhearing her say "I'm glad you keep your word."

Jane quickly walks up the stairs, to avoid her mother seeing her up close. Though as she walks onto the second floor, she is overwhelmed by the obnoxious guitar playing coming from her brother's room. The chords that her brother confuses as the sounds of music, seemingly annoy her to the point she can barely think. It pains her to walk towards his door as his guitar playing gets louder and louder. But she makes it to the door and fiercely knocks on it, getting his attention.

She yells through the door "Other people live here Marcus! Turn it down! Better yet, give up already."

Her brother plays one loud rift and he opens the door to spite her, stringing his guitar and playing any tune that comes to his mind. His hazel eyes and grin get wider with each chord as his sister covers her ears to combat his unfavorable music. As she tries to walk into his room to manually turn down the amplifier, he slams the door shut. Though to her liking, the music lowers and she breathes.

She walks back down the hallway towards her room and is greeted with the beautiful aroma of leftover incense. The smell of lavender mixed with dragon's blood gives her instant relaxation as she places the bag, she got from Tola on her desk.

Jane jumps on her elevated bed feeling comfort in the soft plushness of her periwinkle sherpa comforter. She gazes at the four walls of her room that is painted in periwinkle and dazzled with tapestries and politically artistic posters. She relaxes on her bed and the posters on her wall become tiresome to look at. She turns her attention towards her ceiling and glides her eyes over the transcendent colors of her mandala tapestry. She loves how the array of colors intertwine and how the images capture her mind as well as her sight.

Until she jumps when she hears something hit her window. She quickly looks out to see where the noise came from. And as she looks through the window, another rock hits her window.

Jane opens up her window and says, "Tola. Tola, I know it's you."

The eerie silence of the night captivates her as not a voice, not a sound is heard.

"Tola, I swear, if I have to walk out of this door to get you to stop bothering me. Tola? Tola?"

But Jane doesn't hear anything, only hears the whistling of the wind and the movement of small bushes. The dark shadowy parts of her street make her anxious as she closes her window.

Jane steps away from her window for a moment, trying to see from a distance if she sees anything. But to her surprise, she doesn't see anything until a group of guys walk down the block and Jane turns away from the window.

An incense burns as the strikes of a lighter sounds in her room. She takes hits from her bowl and gazes at her psychedelic posters. It captivates her to the point she feels like it's moving, prompting her to take another hit and lay on her bed and relax. She inhales and exhales as she cracks the window open, trying not to choke on every inhale she takes. Until the smoking becomes mindless and she forgets all about dinner, forgetting her brother's guitar practice and becoming one with the moment.

Jane's mind fades to the man bumping into her shoulder, to the surprise visit from Tola and her ability to look sober in front of her mom. She laughs about the events of the day as it gives her peace that this is how it ended. She places her bowl down and gets comfortable on her bed.

Until a knock is heard on the door.

"Door's open." Jane says.

Billie walks in to see a haze of smoke floating within her room.

"What's that smell? Why is it so smoky in here?" she says, putting her hands on her hips as she waits for a reply.

Jane says, "I'm burning an incense. It helps calm me after school."

"Well you don't need to burn the whole stick, Jane! There can't be that much stress in your life." Billie says as she waives her hand in the air, lifting the incense out of its holder and dabbing the amber out. Jane watches her until she closes her eyes.

Mumbling under her breath "Like you would have any clue about the stresses in my life."

Her mother looks at Jane and says, "Dinner's ready. Don't fall asleep." Billie exits the room as Jane can hear her mother walking back down the stairs.

Jane gets up and says back, "Okay. Okay" before closing the door after her and getting a little snug in the comfort of her bed.

The warm plush covers takes ahold of her as her mind enters into the dream world.

"Jane."

She hears, after having fallen asleep for a few hours. Her eyes open to her empty room but the growling sounds of her stomach begin to fill up the silence. She rubs the crust out of her eyes and wipes the hardened-up drool from the sides of her mouth before making her way downstairs, knowing everyone in the house is in their room and asleep.

Her feet jump at the sudden change in temperature from the wooden floor of the dining room to the cold, ceramic tiles of the kitchen. Her eyes already adjusted to the darkness of the night flinch shut as she opens the refrigerator door. This illuminates the kitchen and a portion of the dining room as she examines the menu of what her mom made for dinner. She takes out a couple of tupperware containers filled with pasta and meatballs. The sight prompts her to gather a plate and silverware to vigorously scoop and scrape as she yearns for the taste and satisfaction of leftovers.

Though eerily in the darkness as her mouth waters at the sight of food, she hears a voice calling out for her.

"Jane. Jane."

Being very confident that everyone in the house is sleeping, she feels a tinge of fear crawl up her spine as she keeps the refrigerator opened and looks around to see anyone near her. She's unable to make out any shapes within the shadow of her house which prompts her to pick up the pace and move towards the microwave.

When she hears the beep of the microwave, she swiftly yet quietly grabs her plate. As the walk towards the stairs becomes a race out of the fright of the night. She glances at every opaque object in sight, making sure there's no one lingering the floors of the house. Once she's back in her room, she immediately starts to scarf down the food on her plate. Until while eating, she hears the voice again, calling her name.

"Jane"

She pauses.

She's stunned from hearing the sound of the voice in her room. As she curiously gets up from her chair and starts looking around to see if there's someone in her room. She checks to see if someone is whispering her name even though there isn't a lot of room to hide.

Jane still sees no figure or object to reference where the voice came from.

"What the...? Is someone there?" Jane says, frantically looking around her room. The room falls silent to Jane painfully listening out for the voice. As she sees nothing around her room, no figure in sight. She slowly sits back down to finish her plate of food. The voice disappears so she chalks it up to be a figment of her imagination. Though she keeps an eye out for any sudden moves or disturbances in her room. Since it didn't come back and she still feels the effects of the high, she assures herself that no one was talking to her and she was just... bugging.

Jane leaves her plate on the desk as she snuggles back in her bed. But as her mind begins to drift when she nudges her head deep into her plush pillow, the voice appears again, forcing Jane to stay wide awake.

It's unfamiliar and indistinguishable to any voice Jane has heard in her life. She never forgets a face or the unique voice of someone she has encountered.

Jane starts to panic because for once, the invisible voice called out a name that wasn't Jane's. To her surprise and fear, the voice answered her and specifically responded

"Call me Alice".

DAY 2

As her eyes roll behind her eyelids and the perception of reality fades into the subconscious mind, flash after flash, breath after breath, she witnesses things that don't pertain to her waking world. The feeling of chains wrapped around her arms. The feeling of chains. She feels it. She stands limp on the cold ground as her shackles keep her balanced. Looking into the abyss of black space in front of her. She screams. A wailing cry.

Only to hear it again.

"Call me Alice."

The answer she had asked for but never in her life expected to receive. So many questions were running through her mind. What is Alice? What does she want?

As she awakens from her dream, sitting at the half table in the corner of the kitchen with a soggy bowl of cereal in front of her. Jane felt so distraught and confused by the incident, sleep was not an option. She roamed endlessly through her mind trying to match the voice to any face she had encountered. She catches herself pacing around the thought of what Alice is, like a caged tiger paces around its cage looking for freedom.

Her eyes crusted over; her hair placed in a messy bun. As her curls spiral and poke out, seeking freedom from the hair tie. She can't stop her mind from racing to explanations that could only make sense to the high or the mentally insane. She would even wait patiently for the voice to speak again and listen for any glimpse of the whispering voice to appear.

But Alice never spoke again for the rest of the night, not a peep heard since the "Call me Alice".

Jane didn't remember her alarm going off, not even the careless attempt of getting dressed and looking presentable for school. The wavy pattern of her hair matches her energy levels and concern for the day. She starts off on an all-time low, only to get lower as the day progresses.

"I hope this day passes by like a thought." she says aloud, unaware of who can hear her.

She looks back towards the dining room to see if anyone did, only to find her mother and father tuned into their needs to start their day. Her mother is checking her emails while sipping on a cup of coffee as her father is indulged in a newspaper article while munching on slices of maple bacon.

Jane always admired the poise her mother had before she went to work. Her normal attire of an all-black skirt suit with her everyday patent leather pumps. The dazzling array of diamonds from the 7 karats in each ear to the canary diamonds in her bracelet, complimented with diamond rings on each ring finger.

A woman of brains and beauty, very gifted at multi-tasking with an addiction to work. She is equipped with the skills to balance work emails on her phone while tying her husband's tie and finding spare moments to eat her granola bar.

Her husband, Isaac, sits next to her and waits for his tie to be tightly knotted, continuing to munch on some bacon and eggs while he enjoys the economy section of The Times. He sports a grey striped shirt with ash gray khakis and patent leather shoes.

They finesse together the aspiration of a comfortable African American family, secure in their finances as they are in their positions at work.

Jane turns away from her parents with a sigh of relief, focusing her attention towards her soggy cereal as she contemplates if she wants to take another bite. Her brother, Marcus walks into the kitchen as he throws his backpack down into the seat next to Jane. He opens the kitchen cabinet to get a cereal bowl, only to close the cabinet and see Jane looking a little jaded this morning. As the younger brother he is to her, he does not hesitate to see a vulnerable moment to insult. So, as he grabs his bowl and fills it up with Honey Bunches of Oats with a sly smile on his face, he dives into the thoughts roaming around his mind about his sister and unleashes the hidden laughter behind his goofy expression.

"Looking a little shabby this morning, I see. Decided to give up before the day even started?"

Jane sighs and tries to dim the argument fueling, saying "Please Marcus, leave me alone. Today is just not the day."

Marcus is tall for his age but consistent with his adolescent built, as he smiles grimly at Jane since he loves to play the part of the annoying brother.

He doesn't back down as he responds "Did you even come home last night? Because you look terrible. You need to stand in front of a mirror and process yourself Jane. Life isn't working for you right now."

Jane painfully tries to keep calm, whispering to him "I'm warning you, Marcus. Don't test me today. You know I came home so shut up."

Marcus smiles as he takes another bite of his cereal. He chuckles to himself thinking of the next comeback to hit his sister with. "Damn, I was hoping those tired eyes and that ratchet hair meant you got some. But you're still bitter, so I guess you just gave up today."

"Marcus." Jane yells back at him. She notices her dad starting to tune into their conversation so she continues in a low tone. "Shut up, Shut up. Not this morning, please shut up."

Marcus sits back in his seat and fingers through his voluminous fro.

He chuckles to himself, unable to resist another comeback. "I wish you did get some Jane. I think that's what you need."

Isaac looks back and says in a stern voice. "What are you too mumbling about?"

He then turns his attention towards Jane, He notices her disarrayed hair and clothes. He says, "Jane, why do you look like that?" As Jane blows it off with her humor and says, "Look like what? A model. Oh...you flatter me too much."

She smooths her hair back as if her dad was implying a compliment.

"Oh... well thanks Pops." She smiles at him as if she's looking into the face of flattery.

"I'm glad someone admires my fashion statement" Jane says. "The 'don't care style' is always trendy."

Her humor does nothing as Isaac remains un-entertained by her antics. He says, "Go fix yourself up before you walk out of my house like that."

Jane rolls her eyes and says in a hush voice "Everyone, and you, can just advert their eyes. I don't care today."

Although Jane thought her last comments were discrete, Isaac walks over to her in anger. And as he stands over her with a stern appearance on his face, he says to her, "This is not a debate or a discussion. I didn't ask you how you felt or if you cared. I told you to fix yourself before you leave my house and that's something you will do before you leave my house."

His large and burly stature starts to present itself. He glazes at her until Jane moves out of her chair as she angrily gets up to do as she was told.

Jane never liked to test her father since his anger could scare the courageous of men with his deep and powerful voice. Though when his children or work didn't piss him off, he became quite the tender-hearted man.

Marcus spoons into his cereal, feeling boastful about what he did and the reaction of his dad. Until Isaac sees the boastful smile on Marcus' face and smacks him on the back of his head.

Marcus is on the verge of tears when he shouts at him "Why'd you do that? I didn't even do anything!"

"Yes, you did! I saw you instigate. You started the whole thing and you need to stop antagonizing your sister so much."

Marcus' heart drops into his stomach as he looks away in shame. He continues to finish his cereal in order to comfort his anger and leave this house sooner.

A few minutes later, Jane comes flying down the stairs as she restarts her day with a fresh, new look. She tries to finish her cereal quickly so she can make the subway on time. She sees her mother leave the house first while their dad waits for Jane and Marcus to finish.

"Can y'all hurry up? You should know my subway leaves before yours. I have to get to work."

The two of them quickly place their empty bowl in the sink before bypassing their impatient Dad and hurrying to catch their subway.

The day proceeds and the long grueling school day begins to present itself; she meets her friends in front of the building before walking in and heading to class.

She says as she walks up to her friend Lianne, "Girl. I have to tell you what happened last night. I don't know if I was tripping or I may actually be losing my mind."

Lianne laughs and says, "You probably were just high. Don't take it too seriously. I have weird experiences all of the time."

Her friend Neal walks up to them with nothing but smiles. He shines his bright white teeth as his light green eyes shine with excitement. He says, "Y'all don't know anything about weird experiences. Have you ever seen a unicorn suddenly walk down the street as you stand naked and a giant is approaching from behind?"

Both of the girls stop and stare at Neal, pondering to see if that was a serious question based off of his experience. Lianne stares at him with her bright blue eyes as her long auburn hair flows gracefully on her white blouse. She places her hand on his forehead and says "Accept yourself. Accept."

There's a moment of dead silence as Neal ponders if she's serious and a tear falls from his eyes. The tension dims as Jane bursts out in laughter, Lianne following after her. The three of them walk into school, Neal recovering from Lianne's comments and says, "Don't do that!"

The school day flies by as she anticipates going home and catching some much-needed sleep. She walks into her home earlier than usual and sprawls out on her bed to gaze deeply at the ceiling.

Her neighborhood hosts a variety of people, stemming from all shades, genders and classes. It's one of the busiest times in her neighborhood to pay attention to all of the people walking down her block and, on the block adjacent to hers.

She says in a smug tone as she observes the men and women dressed in business attire, either returning from work or attending another business function. "Look at these damn penguins. No style. No originality. It's like the individuality gets washed out the older you get."

As she comments like the spectator she is, she pulls out her pipe and reaches for her bottom drawer to grab her Ziploc bag.

The sound of exhalation and coughing fill the silence of her room. As the accumulation of a cloud starts to hover over her bed.

She says as she leans against her window, "This is the life right here. Why choose the ground when you can live in the clouds?"

Jane turns her attention towards the sky as she tries to catch a glimpse of the pastel colored sky. She gazes up at all of the colors in the sky and watches them transform with the setting sun.

The background noise of the city starts to diminish as she finds the sounds of the outside world peaceful. Until her mind drifts to the image of all the people in their suits and ties walking down the block to wherever their destination lies.

Jane says, "Why do we have to be robots? Precise and almost perfect in appearance and way of living. Dressing the way they want you to. Living the life everyone thinks is ideal only feeling a release of pressure when you're on vacation or at happy hour."

"Life."

Jane puts the bowl to her mouth to take another hit until she hears a voice.

Says the kettle calling itself and the world black.

Her heart staggers in fear as she quickly throws the bowl down.

"I got to stop. I don't want to see a unicorn, especially not a giant." Jane begins to cover her head, hoping she doesn't hear a voice. Until it comes back and strikes more fear into her heart.

You talk of conforming to what people want you to be. Living a lifestyle, you think is unwarranted or forced upon. Yet you humbly do it since it is what you seek. Oh Jane, those are choices. No one is telling you how to live.

Jane feels her fear towards Alice turn into confusion, slowly lifting her head up to look around the room.

Jane says "Unseen voice, probably my sanity going down the crazy drain. Please go away, I don't know what you're talking about."

I'm the boogey man coming to get you. Can't you see my teeth? My eerie voice coming to haunt you. Woo.

Jane runs out of her room and screams, "Oh no! I'm becoming like Neal. I'm bugging. I'm going crazy. I got to stop."

She runs down the stairs and patiently waits to see if the voice left. But to her surprise, she hears the voice laughing and realizes that the voice is everywhere she goes.

You slay girl. You slay. How you managed to trick yourself....

Jane says, "Excuse me? I didn't do anything."

Yea you did. But it's all good. You'll figure it out one day.

Jane looks around in confusion and says, "Okay. Okay. Whatever this is, I need it to end. You can't be here."

Jane hears.

I'm sorry but I'm going to be here for a while. You'll need me soon but you just don't know when...

"What does that even mean?" Jane replies in a fury.

She hears.

It's all good. Just relax. Smoke some. You'll be alright.

She says as her emotions start to overwhelm her. "No, I'm not smoking a damn thing." Jane looks around as if she feels her sanity drift away.

"This is crazy. This is absolutely crazy." She says as she takes a deep breath and walks back into her room.

As Jane makes it back into her room, she sits on her bed and tries to tune out the world around her. Though the peace she finds within the solitude of her room begins to cease as she hears footsteps outside of her door.

"Jane!" She hears as her door begins to swing open.

She decides not to answer out of the fear it is Alice again until she hears her name yelled out again and realizes the octave changed.

"Jane!" Marcus yells louder.

"What Marcus? What do you want?"

His important and climatic response turns out to be, "What are you doing?" To which Jane un amusingly says "What does it look like bro?"

"I don't know. It looked like you were kind of sleeping or maybe getting high as a kite. I don't know, just wanted to bother you."

Jane says "Marcus. I am going to need you to close the door. I'm not in the mood to be bothered right now."

He says as he begins to close the door. "It reeks in here. You really need to open a window."

"Maybe you should just get out my room. If you can't handle the stank, hold your breath and leave."

Marcus snickers, "Or maybe, I should just call Mom up here. She can witness this and the stank for herself."

"Marcus, why do you always need to test me? Is this what you wanted? To exercise your most hated quality."

Marcus smiles bright, feeling the need to draw up a bargain.

He says, "Give me a nug and I won't say anything."

His bargain is met with Jane's anger.

"No."

Marcus softly yells, "Mom".

"How about you shove your fist down your throat before I do it? Bet you won't say anything then."

"Keep out of my stash and go away."

She throws a pillow at him to make him close the door quicker, but the action only provokes him to enter in before closing it. He says "If you don't give me a nug, I will call Mom up here right now. And there's no way to get rid of the smoke that quickly for her not to notice."

Jane rolls her eyes at him and moves out of her comfortable position. She sits up and says in a calm but forceful demeanor, "Marcus. You're really trying to piss me off."

He can see the anger increase in her eyes as Jane lays down an ultimatum. Jane lashes at him and says, "You're not the one to hold anyone ransom, especially with the skeletons you have in your closet."

Jane shines him a wicked grin, knowing he can't bet on Jane revealing his secret.

"You're vile." Marcus says. "That game play is really getting old." To which Jane reputably replies, "And yet it still does wonders."

Marcus leaves the room and tells her dinner is ready before slamming the door closed. She listens out to hear his footsteps fade before cracking a window and letting out all of the smoke in her room. She then jumps off her bed and opens all of her windows running along the side of her room before she heads downstairs for dinner.

Walking into the dining room, she sees her mother and brother both quietly sitting at the table. The marble table steams with porcelain trays filled with pot roast and mashed potatoes. The aroma ignites Jane's hunger the moment she walks into the room and encounters the intoxicating smell. Yet her mother and brother whom have been basking in the scent of delicacy are more consumed with the demands of their electronics than the dinner that lies before them.

Jane sits down at the table as her family remains oblivious to her presence across the table. She gazes at them in awe, admiring their ability to border the real and virtual world. Though her patience gets the best of her as the smells of the pot roast begin to torment her growling stomach. And in an instance as her mother and brother remaining subdued by their demanding devices, Jane grabs her fork and starts to fill up her plate.

Her mind becomes encapsulated in the thought of tasting the food, scooping large portions of mashed potatoes and asparagus after loading half of her plate with pot roast. Though her mother and brother remain obsolete to her actions, her father enters the room and questions the urgency of starting dinner.

He says with sarcasm, "You couldn't wait until we say grace?"

"I did wait but Robot 1 and 2 were too busy plugged in. Didn't want to unplug them so I figured why not just fix my own plate", Jane says.

Isaac side eyes Jane as he rubs Billie's shoulder to get her attention.

Marcus awakens in the process as Isaac says, "What happened to no electronics at the table?"

Billie says, "I was waiting for you. I figured, why not do some work while I wait."

Isaac kisses her on her forehead as Jane jumps in and says, "Hey. I was sitting at the table."

Billie looks at her plate in anger, saying "Well, you could have said something. Heathen!"

Jane scrunches her face up and says, "What are we back in the olden days now? Heathen? Really? As if anyone in this family follows the word of God to a T."

Billie says, "Whatever child. You should have said something, especially after I worked hard to make this meal."

Jane says, "I didn't know it was a big deal."

Isaac tries to mediate in order to calm the situation down. He says, "Let's move on. Let's not let a minor issue ruin this family dinner and beautiful spread."

Billie decides to hold her tongue as Jane looks at her mother dauntingly to only ensue the anger between them, aiding in her resilience to abide.

Billie says, "Why are you looking at me like that?"

Jane looks down at her food as her mother fumes in anger.

"I'm telling you, this girl and her attitude! After this beautiful spread that I made for this family. You can't respect that? Then leave this table."

Jane says. "So, you rather have me starve because I filled my plate before you. Why are you acting like this?"

Isaac's eyes speak for themselves as he can feel the anger heating up.

"Now let's act calm and enjoy this dinner", he says.

"Bunch of hypocrites." Jane says under her breath. Though it was loud enough for her parents to hear.

Isaac yells, "That's it! Get up from this table! Now!"

Jane gets up and starts walking towards the stairs.

Billie says as she grabs a couple of slices of pot roast, pressing her fork into them in order to eat her feelings.

"I don't know how we raised such an ungrateful child. It's like they get a certain age where everything we do is just a giant 'screw you' to them."

Isaac tries to calm her down as Marcus remains silent, filling up his plate and trying not to fall into the footsteps of Jane.

Billie continues "I mean we pay a lot of money for that school for her to act like this. She can't even say grace. Won't even speak before starting her dinner? I mean c'mon Isaac. What are we doing wrong?"

Marcus decides to jump in and say, "Well you did just do the same thing."

The room gets silent as Jane stops in her steps as she walks up the stairs.

Marcus continues. "You started filling your plate and we still haven't said grace."

Billie glances at Isaac with a more concerned look as she continues to cut into her food. She says, "You can leave as well."

Marcus looks stunned as he says, "So I can't have an opinion? You did do the same thing."

"Marcus! Either shut up or say grace. I am trying to enjoy the rest of my dinner."

Marcus looks away from his mother as he quickly leaves the table and brings his plate to his room. He leaves Billie and Isaac to enjoy the feast by themselves as Isaac walks into the kitchen to turn on some music and grab a bottle of wine.

Jane looks over the railing to see her mother vent to her dad downstairs. She sees Marcus slam his door shut which only provokes her to do the same.

SLAM!

Jane tries to tune out her parent's muffled discussion which eventually turns into drunken renditions of classic R&B hits. She finishes the food left on her plate and play her own songs to cover up the noise downstairs.

An hour later, Jane walks downstairs to see her parents have left the dining room. She quickly drops her plate into the sink before walking through the dining room and back upstairs into her bedroom. But as she walks upstairs, she hears a tussle in Marcus' room and a large thud. Her curiosity to see what the commotion is provokes her to lightly knock on the door before creaking the door open.

"Hey Marcus. Are you okay?" Jane's eyes widen as she sees Marcus making out with a tall, lean teenage boy. She quickly closes the door as she realized that the other naked man is Neal. She says, "Oh. Sorry. Didn't know someone else was in here."

A smile prompts upon her face as she turns away and thinks to herself, "Neal? Really?"

DAY 3

Jane spent little time getting out of bed and getting ready for the day. Since it's the half-way mark that leads to the promise of the weekend.

She walks towards her closet and says, "What should be the ensemble for this day of fun?" since to her, a day like Wednesday always felt like one of the better days.

Thursday always feels like "close but no cigar" as Friday nights always felt like a moment of bliss. Since Saturday feels like a "Screw it, let's do everything!" type of day while Sunday always felt like a desperate plea for one more day. It's right before the Monday blues and the 'hurry up' Tuesday. The reasons why Wednesday was a choice day; it gives hope.

Jane pulls out her school blazer and slacks as she twists and poises her body to admire her outfit in her body length mirror. She admires the fact that her school uniform colors consist of crimson red, jet black and white as the crimson color always complimented her brown skin tone and made the colors pop even more. She puts on her ensemble for the day and starts to work on her hair.

She frees her untamed, voluminous hair from the compressed form it held while she slept. She strokes her fingers through her hair, moussing her curls and making them more defined. To top off her outfit, she wears her favorite earrings and puts on eye liner before walking out of her room, feeling fresh.

She walks down the stairs confident, making her way through the dining room. She sees her mother and father sitting down at the table as they both read their newspapers under the light of the chandelier. Jane passes by and doesn't say a word. Isaac solemnly glances at her while Billie continues to read her newspaper. He gives her a discontent look before continuing to read his newspaper.

Jane found it unusual that the blinds were closed this morning but figured it was due to the loud renditions of Earth, Wind and Fire she overheard last night. A smile starts to perk upon her face as she sees the two bottles of wine sitting on the kitchen counter, only confirming her ideas as to why the blinds remained closed.

Jane opens up the cherry wood stained cabinets in search for a bowl and box of cereal to get her morning started. She fills up her bowl with some flakes as she grabs a spoon from the dish rack and opens the refrigerator to grab some milk.

"Where's your brother?" Billie asks, looking up over her newspaper after hearing Jane in the kitchen.

Jane says "I don't know. I think he's still in his room."

"Go get him then please. Your father doesn't have a lot time to wait for you too, this morning."

Jane gets frustrated after already pouring the milk over her cereal and loathing the idea of allowing her breakfast to get soggy. She quickly walks up to the stairwell and yells, "Marcus, let's go. We don't have a lot of time in the morning."

"Are you kidding me?" Billie says. The aggravation takes ahold as Jane remembers the wine bottles sitting on the counter.

Billie says, "I could have done that Jane. I asked you to walk up there."

Jane rolls her eyes as she does what she's told to, walking up the stairs to get Marcus from his room. But as she walks up to his door and prepares to knock, the door swings open as Marcus tries to nudge her out of the way.

"Had a good night last night?" Jane asks.

"Better than yours, I bet." he says.

He bolts down the stairs to hurry up and get food into his belly, while Jane follows behind him with a smirk on her face.

He walks past his parents and gives them a half assed smile before fixing his bowl of cereal and sitting at the kitchen table with Jane. Marcus sits in silence as Jane smiles at him with every bite she takes. She feels the need to enact sweet revenge for what happened yesterday morning.

"I see why you were so concerned about me getting some. Now look who's wearing the tired eyes bro."

Marcus quietly replies, "Yes but unlike you, I rock them with pride and I have an excuse."

A sinister smile creeps on her face as she says in a loud tone, "Oh yea Marcus, what's that excuse?"

"What excuse?" Isaac says as he overhears the conversation.

"Marcus is looking a little rough around the edges. Care to share bro, why do you look so tired this morning?"

He stares at her furiously as he says, "Yea, it was all of the loud music last night."

He mouths to her "Shut up" while Jane mouths back "No."

She tries to hold in the laughter as she finishes up her cereal. Marcus maintains a sinister gaze on her as he prays, she gives up.

She says in a low tone, "Why'd you have to pick my friend? Now it's gotta be awkward when he talks about all the play he gets."

"Grow up Jane." he says, though beginning to ponder her last comments.

"What do you mean 'all of the play'?"

Jane laughs as she ignores Marcus and looks at her phone to see the time to catch the subway is nearing.

"Yo, you have to hurry up. We got to go soon." she says as she shows him the time.

They both try to finish before they have to leave for the subway, dashing to the sink before grabbing their coat and walking out of the door.

On the subway, Marcus asks again "Again. What do you mean about all of the play?" Jane smiles as she sees his concerned face reflecting in the window. She says, "Yea, he's not the one to invest a lot of time in if you're looking for something concrete."

The train stops as he says, "Okay, I'm going to need you to just spell it out for me."

Q. IMAGINE

She gets up and places her bag on her shoulder. "Find someone else. He really isn't the one. I mean his perfect hair and good skin makes it really hard to turn away, especially with those eyes. But trust me, you want to turn away. He's not the type to fall in love with."

Marcus replies, "Well, he told me that we were a 'thing' last night so I don't know if what you're saying is sound."

Jae says, "Yea, put a 'no' in front of that 'thing' and you're getting warmer to what he means."

Upon arrival of the school after walking a few blocks from the subway station, Jane and Marcus separate as Marcus goes and meets with his underclassmen inside the school. Jane being an upperclassman meets with her senior friends in front of the red brick Victorian-style school. She scans her eyes over the groups of kids before seeing Lianne and her other friends.

"Another day and more time to waste." Lianne says as Jane nears. She sees their friend Joe trying to mack on Lianne while Neal watches the action.

Lianne says, "Joe, stop. It is way too early for that." She tries to push him away as she looks to her friend Jane to assist. Jane pushes between them as she says "Hey. Stop trying to take my girl. I know those bright blue eyes and red hair make her extremely tempting. But she's spoken for, we solidified it weeks ago"

Joe says, "Yea, you need to quit it. Everyone knows you have a thing for Tola."

Jane looks at him surprised as she says "How do you even know Tola? He doesn't go to this school."

Joe says, "Everyone knows Tola, obviously. His name gets passed around a lot due to his... services."

Jane still grasps Lianne's tall and slender body. She says, "Okay, but that doesn't mean I have a thing for him."

Joe laughs as he starts to fix his white letterhead jacket. The stocky, young man shines a grin on Lianne as he smoothly says, "You got yours Jane. Let me have mine."

Lianne jumps into the conversation and says, "Just because you look like Christopher Reeves prodigal child and we had a 'thing' once. Maybe a few summers ago, doesn't mean I'm yours. You need to chill."

Jane chimes in and says, "Ooo, she told you boy. But I hope that doesn't jeopardize our hookup at your uncle's pizzeria."

Joe fluffs his jacket and says, "You know I'm not petty like that. And we all know you dig me Lianne. Just let me know when you want me. I don't play games."

Lianne blushingly laughs and says, "Yea, we'll see about that."

As Joe walks away, Lianne says "I don't know why he keeps bothering me. We hooked up once last summer and it's been like this since. He needs to move on."

"Maybe it's love." Jane says.

"Maybe it's convenience." Lianne replies.

Neal jumps in and says, "Maybe you just have that magic girl!"

Jane says to Neal, "Yea, you and your magic needs to stay away from my little brother, hoe. Don't start any shit."

Neal laughs, almost falling over. "Girl, I was hoping you would jump in. I could have had both of the McKenzie's."

Jane smiles and says, "Keep dreaming honey. That's the only place where it's going down."

Neal says, "I will and sometimes dreams come true."

Jane and Lianne decide to walk arm and arm together into the school, leaving Neal alone while he gets distracted by a group of attractive girls.

Jane says to Lianne, refocusing on the conversation with Joe. "But really, you must have been doing something right for him. A whole year later and he's still asking for it?"

Lianne laughs off her blushing face and says "Yea, I guess TOO right. Won't leave me alone now, even though we did hook up this summer and a couple of weeks ago."

"Mm hmm. I knew there was something going on between you two. A few summers ago. Well that'll ensure our hookup at Antonio's."

They stroll past the crowd and into the intersection of the halls, still arm and arm until the first bell chimes signaling the start of first period.

"Meet you at the back entrance for lunch?" asks Lianne as she draws her arm from Jane's.

Jane shrugs and says, "Sure we can do that. I think Roscoe and the gang want to meet at the back gate for our "usual".

Lianne chuckles with delight, "Sounds good to me. Perfect day for some herbal therapy."

"Lianne, every day is a good day for some herbal therapy."

Jane begins to head towards the south hall of the intersection.

"Only to you Jane. Your crazy girl." says Lianne, who walks in the opposite direction.

And as the two girls part ways, feeling the need to head to class so they're not too late.

Jane sarcastically yells out to Lianne, "I'm the sane one if I can admit we all need therapy."

"True. See you then." Lianne says before running off to class.

Jane knows the distaste her first period teacher has for tardiness and herself in particular, so she prepares for the snickering comments he will give her upon her arrival to English class.

The old and dated man, stooped from many years of writing and bitter with age and loneliness, glares at Jane with detest as he watches her stroll into class and settle in towards the back of the class.

Mr. Dimonte was once an eloquent and influential writer during his younger years but instead of spending his time writing more novels or love haikus, he spends his time reading old Victorian-style writings at cafes and bistros.

Mr. Dimonte has always detested Jane in particular, for her lack of respect on any figure who tries to control her or her tardiness.

Her constant demonstration that she could care less about his feelings always conflicted with his unyielding attitude; bringing about a little feud.

"Well I guess it's time for me to start this lesson, now that everyone is finally here. Thank you, Jane, for deciding to make an appearance." His voice grown hoarse over the years due to heavy tobacco use. Jane flashes him a half assed smile before looking out of the window, trying to avoid the glare that she feels Mr. Dimonte give her.

"I hope everyone did the writing assignment last night", the teacher says. "I look forward to seeing what you guys have come up with."

He says, "I've recently thought of the idea that instead of having you guys just hand the assignment in, I'm just going to have you guys recite your work and then place it into the bin on my desk."

Most of the class shows panic on their faces by the blindsided assignment. Jane looks unamused because she knows this teacher loves to pull the wool over people's eyes.

One of the students, class valedictorian elect Monica Gonzalez, starts to question the reason for this addition to their assignment. She says politely, "Mr. Dimonte, don't you think this is a little short notice for that? I mean, what if I wrote something that isn't meant to be read in front of class?"

Mr. Dimonte rolls his wrinkly eyes, unphased by the pleads of his students. He says, "Ms. Gonzalez, if you have written something that cannot be expressed verbally due to the content of it then you should have picked a different topic. This is a creative writing class, not a Catholic confession."

A hush starts to fall over the class with the exception of the occasional chuckles and whispers as Mr. Demonte asks for volunteers saying, "Who would like to share first?"

With a few minutes passing and not a stir nor sound in the classroom, Mr. Dimonte says, "Alright. I guess I'm going to have to start calling on people since no one wants to volunteer."

His eyes scan over the room looking for the perfect person to pick. But his eyes stop and a smile brightens on his face as he looks towards Jane.

"Ms. McKenzie, how about you do the honors of starting us off. Since you arrived late and last in class, you should be the first to read your assignment."

Jane looks over at Mr. Dimonte. She figures it was a matter of time since she did come late to class. She proudly stands up with her assignment in hand and begins to explain her work, while standing in front of her desk.

"I titled this work, Sally and the Stone." she says.

"Is this a story of a poem? asks Mr. Dimonte.

"It's a little bit of both. A story that rhymes pretty much."

The class chuckles before falling silent to Mr. Dimonte's gaze as he soon after motions to Jane to begin to read her assignment.

Jane begins.

>Sally girl had a mind of her own.

She hated being at home and hated being alone.

In a house full of warmth, she grew up cols,

And time after time, her heart grew to stone.

She met a man. A handsome man,

A man whose warmth reached out like hands.

She loved this man and he loved her too,

Yet Sally's heart was still stone, there was no breakthrough.

He tried his best by showering her with affection,

Giving her everything. All of the love and attention.

Yet nothing could warm up Sally's cold heart.

She was nothing but a vessel and she knew it from the start.

Until Sally woke up in the middle of the night,

She looked to her side and turned on the light.

She saw not a person, but a note with a stone.

And as she moved the small stone, she found out why she's all alone.

The note said: "Sally, you know I will always love you.

And time after time, I will think of you.

But I can't bare the unpleasant cold you hold,

As I've tried to warm you up but my dear you have no soul.

Your soul matches this stone so keep it close, don't let it go,

Maybe this is what you need. Some time alone to grow."

She thought about weeping but those tears were hard

to find.

She thought about sleeping yet there was no silencing her mind.

She's doesn't understand why he left so insincerely,

They didn't have the chance to talk which is leaving her kind of leery.

But she turns her attention turns towards the stone, feeling its cold, smooth tone.

She picks it up and feels the story rattle to her bone.

It's ridges and smooth sides, produced beautifully over time.

Its ocean blue exterior making Sally feel sublime.

And for the first time in her life, she felt a connection,

Not love, not passion but an understanding in essence.

But Sally was all alone. She had nothing but the stone,

Yet she got the time she needed to grow and become whole on her own.

She got the time to figure out who she is and who she will become,

To love herself for being unique and an imitation of no one.

"Excuse me Ms. McKenzie, but how much longer is this story?" Mr. Dimonte says.

Jane, annoyed by his comments, sits back down in her seat and says, "It's done. I'm finished now."

"No, I don't think you are Ms. McKenzie. Your rhythmic poem story, whatever was nice but I'm going to have a few comments of improvement for it. Who's next?"

"Can't really grade creativity, jagoff." Jane says under her breath.

Unaware the old professor heard her, she is caught off guard when he walks up to her desk giving her a reproachful look.

"What did you just say, Ms. McKenzie?"

"Say when?" she replies.

Q. IMAGINE

Mr. Dimonte says in a loud stern voice, "What did you just say to me Ms. McKenzie? Right after I gave your feedback."

"I said thank you for the feedback." Jane playfully smiles at her teacher in an attempt to dull the situation. Her classmates start to snicker and avoid Mr. Dimonte's glare when he turns around impatiently. He overhears the side talk.

"You need to be wise and more careful with that mouth of yours", he angrily says.

"Sir, I promise you I wasn't being a wise ass."

The class begins to laugh even harder as Mr. Dimonte's anger intensifies.

"One more comment and you're out of here Ms. McKenzie! I promise you!"

Jane decides to remain silent as he sits back down, catching his breath from pacing around the class. He turns his attention towards the other students insisting upon continuing the oral assignments. "Now who wants to go next? Don't make me call on someone." he announces.

Half of the class reads their assignments for the remainder of the period, in which Jane silently stares out the window, uninterested and inattentive to the teacher and her classmates. Mr. Dimonte distastefully glances at Jane for the rest of the class. He avoids confrontation by keeping his glances short and trying to focus his attention to the class entirely. When the class bell rings signaling the end of the period, Jane swishes in between classmates to avoid being singled out by Mr. Dimonte and held after class.

Jane moves from class to class each one lasting 45 minutes. Her mood and energy become more tiresome and lethargic by each class bell signaling either the starting or the ending. By the time she enters her math class, she has lost complete interest in anything school related. Her only focused was on her next period which happens to be lunch. The impending freedom of the next 30 minutes gives her a boost in moral to push through the last two classes. While she counts the minutes down, showing no interest in the teacher's lecture or the engagement of the class. She stares outside of the window, patiently waiting to hear the bell ring.

But when that bell rings...

"DING!"

Jane leaves as the teacher says, "Okay class, make sure you finish the 3 pages of absolute values due tomorrow. This will be a graded assignment."

The students rush through the door, creating the wave of people trying to squeeze in between the doorway. Jane quickly drifts towards the side of the crowd, sliding through the sliver of space between the doorway and the other students trying to gain entrance into the hallway. She holds her bag in front of her when moving through crowds. In order to prevent her bag getting caught on someone else and holding her back.

Once free from the accumulation of students now plaguing the hallway, either searching for their next class or convening with friends. Jane walks towards the back entrance of the school to meet Lianne, Roscoe and Neal for her lunch break.

"Who's that sexy mama walking this way?" says Neal, sashaying towards Jane.

"You sway those hips like you want something girl."

Jane plays along and starts to accentuate her hips even more. "Aye, you got something I want Neal?"

"I got a whole lot girl! Let me know"

"Damn Neal, you really do want both McKenzie's. You can't just have one?", Lianne says, stepping into the conversation.

"I like everybody. That is part of my problem." Neal says boastfully.

A tall lanky guy wearing a black crew neck sweater, beige khaki pants and red sneakers, stands up from leaning on the back gate demonstrating his height and throws his long black dreads with gray tips in a bun.

"Don't you think it's time to go guys? Lunch period doesn't last forever."

Lianne agreeing with Roscoe says, "Yea I think we should head over now."

Jane has been looking forward to this moment all day. She starts to skip through the entrance gleefully as she says, "I want to reach heights today guys."

"During lunch period?!", Lianne says hastily.

"Yea Jane, you're going from enthusiast to straight up stoner status. We need to at least not draw attention to each other." says Neal.

"Agreed." Roscoe says.

Jane says, "We'll see."

They each walk out of the gate, making it down the block and then crossing the street together. They head a little further down the block, opposite the street of the school. They head towards an Indian style restaurant and lounge called Uncle Sook's.

As Neal leads the group through the restaurant, passing the restaurant area and through a part of the lounge. They head to a private area near the kitchen that's hidden in ruby style beads. They push the beads away and enter a small and dark room that centers a tall hookah on a round table. The room is lined with cushions like a booth so each member finds a spot around the hookah, making sure Neal is sitting at one of the edges.

As soon as they settle in, an older man wearing an apron pushes through the beads in a haste. He analyzes all of their faces looking for a familiar one. The dim lighting makes it hard for him to see who sits before him. But his eyes finally rest on a familiar face closest to the door. His demeanor calms as he says in a joking manner, "So the gangs meeting on a Wednesday now?"

"Yea Uncle Sook. We switched the days this week. Is that okay?" Neal says.

"Yea that's fine with me. No one saw you come in here. I only knew someone was back here because the beads were moving. Just let me know ahead of time when you guys switch days. Okay?"

The groups say okay and nods in unison. Uncle Sook steps out of the room for a second and comes back with a jar of tobacco, coals and menus.

"You guys know the deal. $25 each for the hookah and food.

Only order from the lunch menu", he says.

The group nods again in agreement as he proceeds to set up the hookah for them. Once done, he tells them to enjoy and leaves the room.

The moment he leaves, Roscoe and Neal both stand up and begin to remove the hot coals and foil off the hookah. Roscoe digs into his pocket and takes out a bag filled with herb. He breaks the herb over the tobacco while Neal keeps an eye out for Uncle Sook. Once done they put everything back together and get ready for their smoke session.

"Who wants first hit?"

"You take it Neal, for constantly hooking us up with this spot. Who knew your uncle would be so chill about us smoking back here." Roscoe says.

"Yea the hookah part he's chill about. It's legal at 18 in my parent's country." Neal says.

"The weed however needs to stay hidden." He takes the hose and starts filling up his lungs. He turns on the vents before exhaling, producing a whirlpool effect due to the vents. The smoke funneling into the vents looks magical within the dim lighting of the room and the rhythmic sounds of the carnatic music. The soothing sounds of a flute playing against the strings of the tampura, enhance the aura of serene tranquility with each puff everyone takes.

Their bodies begin to relax as their minds drift out of their bodies. The only relief from their subconscious world is the gentle tap of a hand passing them the hose. The hose circles around the table, each rotation feeding the dancing cloud. And as the rotation slows down, the cloud dissipates.

"I think it's done." says Neal. He leans back to rest his head on the lounge cushion.

Lianne sighs and says, "Thankfully" As she slumps back into her lounge chair.

Their eyes can barely see each other as they all dim from the haze.

Jane tries to mutter in over the music, "How much time do we have until the period ends?"

But Roscoe and Neal look to the ceiling as Lianne looks at Jane in a daze.

"Did you say something?"

She speaks in slightly louder tone. "Yea. How much time do we have until the period ends?"

Lianne turns to her phone to check the time and tries to figure out an answer for her friend. "I think we have about 15 minutes, give or take."

"We should order something to eat", says Jane.

"So, we have enough time to eat before we leave."

Neal overhears and takes his phone from his pocket and says, "Place your orders."

While Neal texts everyone's orders to Uncle Sook, Lianne leans over to Jane and asks.

"Jane, did you hear about the party this weekend?" Though Jane remains oblivious to her words.

In a louder voice, she says, "Jane. Are you going to the party this weekend?"

Jane looks at Lianne and says, "What party?"

"The party Joe is throwing at his house this weekend since his parents are away on a business trip."

"No, he didn't tell me about it. When is it?" says Jane.

"It's this Friday. Two days. It's supposed to be a themed party like a Luau or Beach themed, because it's the last days of official summer."

Neal laughs. "Yea it definitely doesn't feel like summer. Hopefully it's an indoor party."

"It is. At least that's what he told me." says Lianne. "He said everyone's invited so it should be fun."

"I'm down to go." says Neal.

"Second that." says Jane.

"I already knew about it" Roscoe says.

"Nobody asked if you knew Roscoe. She only asked if you were going" Jane says.

"No, she didn't." Roscoe says defending himself.

 "She didn't ask anything."

"Whatever Roscoe. Are you going?" asks Lianne.

"Obviously. I'll be there", he says with a smile. "I just love messing with y'all duo. Always tag teaming."

Jane and Lianne look at each other in agreement while the beads start to shift and Uncle Sook comes in with trays of food. Neal takes the money from each one of them and gives it to his uncle while he simultaneously hands him the trays to disperse to them.

They all take mouthfuls of rice and chicken biryani; Jane asks Neal for a time check to see how much quicker she has to eat. He tells her they have a little less than 5 minutes till they have to start walking back. And with that notification, everyone begins to eat faster so they don't have to carry the food back into school. The smell of smoke on their clothes along with Uncle Sook's logo on the bags of food would notify the school of his establishment and how he allows them to smoke there.

"Alright, we got to go." says Neal.

Everyone stands to their feet stretching and burping after speed eating their meals. They walk out of the beads towards the back door passing Uncle Sook in the kitchen. The group thanks him for his generosity and bids him farewell before they leave.

"Okay guys. Let's act cool." Lianne says.

The gang smiles, grinning from ear to ear in the bliss of the high. Their sunglasses hide their hazy eyes but their smiles and aroma speak for them as they walk down the sidewalk.

Jane says, "I'm always cool. That's just me, no need to act."

"Maybe we should spray." Lianne says as she notices the smell.

Q. IMAGINE

"Be cool." says Roscoe. "If we act like we don't care, then people won't draw attention to it."

Lianne asks, "Where did you hear that, Roscoe?"

"Lianne, some things you just need to live... to know."

"So..." Neal chimes in and says, "Does that mean it works or is this the practice of your philosophy?"

Roscoe laughs and says, "Either way I'm practicing. I'm practicing what I speak on in this exercise of life."

"You and these philosophies Roscoe. I need facts because getting caught is real."

"Lianne, I have some spray if you want." Jane says, coming to the rescue. "I have a free period after this so that's why I'm not as cautious."

"Yea I made need some too." Neal says.

Jane laughs.

"It's Victoria's Secret."

"So..I don't mind smelling beautiful. It's everybody's type." he replies.

Roscoe says, "Whatever guys. I understand the philosophy isn't for everyone."

"Roscoe, your philosophy only works because you've been smoking since the 9th grade. If the staff of this institution don't know about you already, they never will."

Roscoe says, "It could be that donation my father gave to the school or they could have just embraced the stereotype that I am the next best rapper."

The group continues to laugh and joke on all the high things Roscoe says. After drifting back down from the cloud and onto campus, they part ways and head to their next period.

Jane enters the prestigious library of the school, walking past the vast aisles of mahogany book shelves and the Mac filled computer rooms. She walks up the stairs to the second floor which is mainly for quiet studying and work. She normally uses this time to work on her classwork but due to the amount of herb she just inhaled, her primary focus is taking a nap before her next classes.

She sits down at one of the corner desk near the far end of the library, lifting her bag on the desk to enact as a temporary pillow. She tries to get comfortable and let her mind drift, nudging her head into her bag and pretending it's one of the soft pillows on her bed. Though instead of her mind being at rest, thoughts and words start to soar through and inspire her to write down a few phrases.

> "Dazed and confused,
>
> Is it a movie or my mood?"

She laughs as she feels the words and phrases flow through her pen.

> I can't see the truth,

Since it lies in thoughts that are rued.

My secrets hide,

Only a select have the ability to confide.

To understand where my truth lies,

And distinguish what's truth and what's a lie.

She sighs as she feels the depth of her heart spill into the words to come.

My soul is chained, only writing keeps my thoughts free,

My words are misunderstood until they stain the pages and set me free.

My thoughts can be deeper than a black hole or as shallow as a creek,

And if you don't agree with that, well...then you never really heard me speak.

Say my name if you only speak it with eloquence,

Tell me you love me if it originates from your heart,

Love can be an eternal flame to illuminate souls from the dark,

And protect unity from pure decadence.

You can touch me, you can love me, just don't leave me when you're done,

You can need me, and if you teach me, show me how to be with someone.

Persuade me, engage me, tell me what you're thinking,

Fly high with me, run the skies with me, let me know when you're sinking,

Hopefully you can understand me,

Hopefully you can stay and be family to me.

Q. IMAGINE

> Open my mind and look at my dreams,
>
> Tell me what you see.

She puts her pen down now feeling the serene silence in her mind. She lays her head down and tries to catch some sleep for the remainder of the free period...until Alice comes back.

Jane.

"Shut up." she says with her eyes closed.

Jane.

She tries not to get annoyed and makes it her mission to be engaged in falling asleep. She tunes out every voice, inside and out that she hears. The only thing she acknowledges is how good it feels to lay on her bag and sleep.

Time passes as Jane lifts her head off of her backpack, feeling she has been asleep for quite some time. She looks down at her phone and sees that she missed her home economics class and there's ten minutes left in her business class. The last class of the day.

"Oh, shit!" she says. She wipes the dry drool on her cheek and crust out of her eyes.

Jane stands up and stretches to see the library is completely packed with teachers. She ducks down before any of them could see and decides to wait in the library until the last bell rings.

Once the bell rings and the teachers disperse, she leaves the library and heads towards the front entrance of the school.

From the entrance of the school, she walks down the block from the school to a pizza spot. Coincidentally, hearing her friends call her from up ahead.

On the days they smoke, the gang always stops by the pizza parlor and grabs a slice before heading home. As they walk through the glass door of the pizza parlor, Jane spots Tola sitting down and eating a slice.

"Tola!" she shouts.

Liane, Roscoe and Neal chime in as chorus, shouting his name.

Jane goes to sit down at his table while everyone else walks to the register to order. Her backpack squishing up against her back while she sits down to chat.

"Tola, what brings you here?" she says.

"Pizza" he mutters as he stuffs the slice in his mouth. The greasy juices squirt out of the bread and drip the cheese and sauce all over his plate.

"What are you doing for the rest of the day?" she asks him.

He smiles and looks up at her, "Nothing. Do you want to go for another walk tonight?"

She smiles and says, "Sure we can go for a walk tonight. Do you want to hang with all of us right now though? Like we're just going to walk around and smoke some more after we eat our pizza."

Tola finishes his slice and wipes his mouth trying to conceal his smile. He says "You know I'm always down to smoke, Jane. But I can't right now. I'm here for business."

Roscoe overhears their conversation and shouts out. "Speaking of business, I could use some extra. Especially for this walk."

Tola says as he sees the cashier starting at all of them, "C'mon man. Don't make it so hot. I got you, just be cool."

Though Tola can feel the energy from the cashier as he stares at him in disgust when he rings up Neal and Roscoe. Tola gets annoyed and storms out of the pizza parlor. He gives Roscoe a dirty glare before he opens the door to leave and sees Jane.

He says, "Just text me when you want to walk or meet me outside of your house. The same time as a couple of days ago. I'll be there."

Tola leaves as Roscoe is surprised by his abrupt departure.

Roscoe says, "What was his problem? I didn't even say anything that loud."

Roscoe angrily biting into his slice of pizza as Jane observes Roscoe tear into his slice.

She says "You did make it a little conspicuous. You should know how Tola is. He's always been on edge, especially when he's holding."

"You'd think someone who smokes so much wouldn't have an opportunity to be tense. But I guess it all just depends on the person" says Roscoe while taking another bite out of his slice.

"Shut up Roscoe. You made it obvious and that's why he got

mad. He was probably meeting someone here." Jane snaps back at him.

"And look at you, defending your man", says Neal as he sits next to Roscoe.

Jane rolls her eyes and gets up from the table to order food.

"Hey Jane!" Neal shouts.

Jane continues to ignore him.

Neal shouts her name in the background and Jane tries to start a conversation with Lianne in order to tune him out.

"What did you order?" Jane says to Lianne.

"Just a regular slice. Nothing special. I'm just going to hook it up though! With some garlic and parmesan…"

"Damn, that sounds good. I might have to do that too.", says Jane.

"You're going to eat garlic?", asks Lianne.

Jane replies, "Yea I love garlic."

Lianne says "Oh, I thought since you're going to see Tola tonight, you would want to keep your breath fresh."

"Not you too Lianne", Jane says frustratingly. "We're just friends that kick it sometimes. Nothing else. Nothing more."

Lianne says as she smiles. "Yea, okay Jane. It's like the same with me and Joe?"

"No. Not the same."

Jane begins to hear Neal again shouting her name so she tunes him out trying not to let him get under her skin. Although Jane begins to get successful at that attempt, the man behind the register begins to make it a problem as he angrily looks at Lianne and Jane.

"Excuse me young ladies." he says. "But could one of you answer him so he shuts up? Today."

Quickly, Jane turns around and yells, "Shut up Neal!"

The cashier's face turns red and flustered as he slams his cash register and quickly bags Lianne's slice.

"Okay here's your slice. Now all of you get out of my establishment. Right now!" he says.

Jane looks at him and says "But I wanted to order too. You told me to answer him so I did."

He glares at Jane and yells "Yea, I told you to answer him, not scream bloody murder. Go somewhere else!"

He then pushes the white paper bag towards Lianne and tells them again to leave.

Jane storms out the pizza place alone and infuriated. Lianne follows along with Roscoe and Neal.

"Jane, wait up!" Lianne says as she tries to catch up.

Jane slows down but still looks pissed off about not getting her slice.

"You okay?" asks Lianne.

"Girl, I need to get some food before I kill Neal." says Jane as she glares into the distance.

Lianne says to her, "Okay. Okay. If you still want pizza, we can go to Antonio's."

Jane then nods her head and says, "Take me there".

The two girls keep walking until Lianne nudges Jane to turn right. Turning on a block, they see a sign saying "Pizza" and a line heading out of the door.

Jane stops in awe.

"I have to wait on that line?", she asks.

Lianne smiles and says, "Girl, stop. You know Joe works here."

They continue to walk a few steps towards the restaurant when Lianne pulls Jane to the side of a brick building and starts texting on her phone. Once she's done, she gives Jane the head nod and tells her to wait a few minutes. After the line starts to die down, they see Joe in a pizza apron come out of the restaurant holding a small pizza box and heading towards them.

Joe meets up with the girls and hands Jane the pizza box. He hands it to her and quickly looks back to gauge how the line is before hugging Lianne. Before he runs back to the restaurant, he smiles at Jane and says, "I better see you now at my party tomorrow night."

Jane shrugs her shoulders and smiles, saying "We'll see. But Joe, how do you even find the time to work?"

He laughs as he runs back into the restaurant and says "I'm a man on a mission. A jack of all trades. I better see y'all there."

Jane opens up the box and sees two large slices goldenly encrusted in mozzarella cheese. As soon as she opens up the box, the smells and heat overwhelm her. She lifts up a slice, almost burning her fingers off. And as she bites into it, she greets her taste buds with the savory taste. It quenches her delightful palate as she finishes off one slice and closes the box to save the other.

"Good, isn't it?" asks Lianne.

Jane looks at Lianne with gratitude. She nods her head in agreement and continues to walk with her friend.

Jane looks at the time and says "Damn, I have to go. The last subway before the time we meet leaves in twenty minutes. I have to hurry since the station is a few blocks away from here."

Lianne replies, "Okay. That's cool with me. I'm probably going to walk back and wait for Joe. He told me he should be off in a couple of hours."

"You're going to stay there for a couple hours?" Jane asks.

Lianne smiles as her cheeks start to blush. "Yea girl, why not? I mean.... he gives me free pizza and this parlor has a mini arcade. Why not?"

Jane shrugs her shoulders and says, "Yea. I understand why'd you want to stay. Free pizza says enough."

She hugs her friend as they bid farewell and Jane runs off to the station. She dodges people from left to right, jumping down the steep stairs to get to the station. She swiftly slides her card through the card swipe and hops on the train before it leaves.

As she gasps in relief for making it, as sweat drips down her face.

As she's sits on the train waiting for her stop, she can't help but think about her friends and Tola. She thinks to herself in disbelief on the fact that her friends think her and Tola are more than just friends.

Until.

Jane sees eyes upon her and they linger as the train stops at each stop. She gazes over at a man in dirty clothes sitting a few feet away from her.

His smile looks familiar though his face is hidden behind dirt and old hat. He hides his face from her sight as Jane questionably glares at him.

She gets flustered and starts to rub her head from track of thoughts spinning in her brain. She shakes her hair in an attempt to cut that train of thought off from her mind and start to think about Joe's upcoming party.

As the subway stops again, and the man quickly exits leaving behind an old newspaper article.

Jane tries to sidetrack her thoughts and brush off the stranger's alarming gaze. Until her stop comes and she walks past the newspaper article. She doesn't see much in her gaze other than the crumples up words of "MISSING".

Tola leans next to a tree near Jane's house, patiently waiting. He repeatedly checks his phone for a text and gazes down the block to see if she's coming. To his surprise, he sees her from afar. As an out of breath Jane sits on her stairs and tries to catch a few gulps of air.

Tola looks at her and laughs.

"Why were you running?"

Jane tries to catch her breath and say, "I didn't want to make you wait so long. I knew you were already upset."

She leans back against the concrete stairs and tries to relax.

"I'm sorry. I forgot to look at my clock when I left the pizza parlor."

He sits down next to her and admires her for trying to catch her breath. He says "Jane, you didn't have to run. I would have waited here."

Jane looks at him and says, "Really? Even like an hour later?"

Tola looks away and smiles, "You have to come home, right? You shot me a text saying you were going to be late."

She laughs and starts to bring herself to her feet.

"You have a point", she says.

He pulls a cannon out of his pockets and shuffles in his back pocket for a lighter.

"Dude", she says as her eyes widen. "Well I'm definitely skipping dinner tonight."

"How are you even thinking about food with a pizza box in your hand?" Told asks.

"You saw my eyes earlier and now question my hunger when you pull out a cannon? How am I supposed to quench this when there so much green floating around?"

Told says, "You have a point." As he flicks the lighter and begins to cherry the cannon.

The two start to smile down the block as they engage in conversation and smoking.

Jane takes a few hits and hands it back to Tola. She asks, "So…. are you going to Joe's party tomorrow?"

He pulls the cannon from his lips and says, "I thought you already asked me that at the pizza parlor."

Jane says "I don't know. Or I don't remember. I got so pissed off after you left, anything before Neal being an embarrassment spaced from my mind."

"What happened?", he asks.

Jane says, "Neal was being an idiot saying things along the line of me defending you and us becoming close."

"So, you defended me?" He asks as he blows the smoke from his mouth.

Jane already knows where the conversation is heading so she tries to downplay what happened.

"It wasn't a defend. It was more of a stand up for the truth. Don't take it personal."

His normal grin that stays on his face diminishes and turns grim. He doesn't look at her and just passes the cannon to Jane and they continue walking in silence to her house.

"So, was that a yes or no to Joe's party?" she says trying to change the subject.

Tola looks down at his phone and says in short "We'll see".

Jane can see the hurt in his eyes and which makes her feel bad.

"So, having a sharp tongue is one of the key traits in my personality. I hope you're not offended because 1. It wasn't intended and 2. I can't help my nature."

His grim face turns into a smile as he laughs at her wit. Jane feels relieved with the presence of his smile, saying, "I told you. Your honesty is what I love about you."

"So that's twice you haven't given me an answer for the one question I asked you", she says.

Tola smiles and says, "I did answer that question the very first time you asked me. You can't blame me for your lack of memory."

Jane pushes him to where he almost trips into a tree and falls over. They both begin to laugh as they reach Jane's front door.

"Last time. Take it or leave it." Jane says.

Tola smiles. "Take what?"

"Take the option to answer my question." Jane replies.

Tola gives her a warming hug and then steps down onto the sidewalk. He says looking up to her now "You'll see soon enough. Two more days, right?"

"Okay. Two more days. Thanks for tonight." she says.

"You're welcome."

"See you in two more days."

Tola laughs as he begins to distance from the door. "No promises."

Jane walks into the house and avoids her family sitting at the kitchen table eating. She walks up the stairs and can feel her family's eyes glaring into her skull from behind. She walks into her room and closes her door.

DAY 4

And all I see are chains and a dark room. As I call out,

Alice

Alice

Jane wakes up in a fog, as her mind continues to float around in the clouds. The hookah session with her friends brought her up to that level, but the after school walk with Tola is keeping her there. She gets up and looks at herself in the mirror as she sees her eyes look hazier than ever, turning away from her image and starting to reminisce on her friend's insinuation. The idea that her friendship with Tola is something more than platonic.

"Yea, I always knew he had a thing for me. But I never really paid it attention because I knew I didn't like him. I do enjoy his company and conversing with him. He is a good-looking guy. Do I really want to take it there?"

"Why am I even thinking of this? Maybe he's thinking of me." A smile perks upon her face as she reaches into her closet for her uniform. She says, "Maybe he is thinking of me right now and that's why I'm thinking of him. Ugh, I wish I knew. I just don't know. Maybe he'll go to the party."

After getting ready, Jane walks down towards the kitchen. Her mind still floats in the clouds so she doesn't even hear or entertain her brother's early morning shenanigans. Her mind is completely within her thoughts and focused on the subject of Tola until she finishes her cereal and her father starts to get ready to head to the station.

"You guy's ready?" Isaac asks as he takes his coat off of the rack.

Marcus answers 'yes' while Jane remains deaf to his words so he nudges her to get her attention.

"Jane, you ready."

"What?" she asks.

Marcus begins to laugh. He answers for her as he side eyes her, seeing the pinkish tint to her hazel eyes.

"You smoke too much."

"Man, shut up. You need a better hobby." Jane says in an annoyed tone as she walks towards the coat rack.

Jane and Marcus walk down the sidewalk, heading towards school after getting off of the subway. He sees Neal along with Roscoe and Lianne and starts to wave at him in order to get his attention.

Jane sees her brother's desperate attempt for his attention and quickly walks ahead of him, saying "Yea, good luck with that."

Q. IMAGINE

Marcus rolls his eyes as he waits for Neal to looks his way. Neal finally turns his attention towards Jane, seeing Marcus waving at him and smiling in the corner of his eye. He looks hesitant to even give Marcus another glance, settling for a quick wave and then turning his body in the other direction.

Jane walks up to him and says, "Wow, you can't even say hi anymore." As Neal tries to blow off her comments by saying, "He's not my boyfriend and I like to keep a low profile."

Jane says with sarcasm, "Yea, when it's your convenience. There's was nothing low about what you did at the pizza parlor yesterday." Jane walks away as she looks back to see Marcus, holding back the sour feelings as he consoles himself with his friends.

She turns back around and walks up to Neal, saying "Please leave my brother alone. If you don't have the heart to be with him then stay away and don't get me involved."

Jane turns away as Lianne reaches out to her. Neal snaps on her and says, "I do what I want. To whomever I want. You should stop acting like your boss."

His comments only ignite Jane as she moves her hand from Lianne and slaps Neal across his face.

"When my brother's feelings are involved, I am boss. I am telling you what to do. You think you can hurt my brother and I'm not going to do anything about it? No. Leave him alone."

Marcus sees Jane furiously yelling at Neal from a distance as the slap draws attention to everyone outside of the school.

Neal tries to charge towards her as Roscoe holds her back, Lianne pushing in between them.

She says before she walks away, "I don't even know why I hang with you. You're nothing but scum."

"You're a royal bitch. I can't wait for this year to be over so I don't have to see you or your pathetic brother."

Neal moves Roscoe's hands from his blazer as he turns around to walks away, seeing Marcus with a look of disgust. Marcus rolls his eyes as he avoids Neal's gaze, prompting Neal to shove people away as he enters the school building.

Jane tries to walk into the school building but is stopped by a tall and husky man, wearing a black suit and tie with the gold name plate with the title 'Superintendent'. He whisks her away and says, "I think you know what this is for." Attempting to pull her arm away as they both walk arm and arm into the building.

All day, Jane sits in a quiet room of the library, using the time she has to make-up for the work she missed yesterday. The librarian enters the room periodically, instructing her on her next assignments and handing them out. As Jane counts the minutes away until the day is over. Her lunch period is consumed of handling assignments and tasks, barely having enough time to walk to the cafeteria to get something to eat. She enters back into her quiet room as she sees more assignments on her desk.

"Damn. I really have been slacking lately." As she takes a couple of bites and gets back to work.

Until she hears a voice.

Was that slap for you or in defense of Marcus?

Jane pauses mid-way into biting her sandwich. She looks around and sees the librarian reading a book, feeling the need to answer this still mysterious voice.

"Hey. You've been quiet lately so maybe we should keep things that way."

Hey. I'm just here to help your ass out. You know the saying, "Don't know what you've got till it's gone.

"I'll take my chances."

The librarian clears her throat in order to warn Jane to be quiet. Glancing into the quiet room to see who Jane is talking too. Jane smiles as she signals, she's just speaking aloud on her assignments, watching the librarian look away as she tries to console herself.

She says in a whisper, "I'm ignoring you."

Can't be ignoring me if you're still talking to me.

She takes a deep breath as she tries to focus on her work, tuning out every voice or sound she hears in the quiet room.

After classes end and the librarian tells her she can leave for the day, she decides to walk straight home since she still needs to catch up on her work. She walks towards the subway station and sees Marcus walking that way as well. She calls out to him as she tries to catch up but his pettiness kicks in as he refuses to walk next to her. He walks in front of her or behind, doesn't even acknowledge her when they sit on the train.

She says, "Marcus, why are you mad?"

Marcus pretends that he didn't hear her as he starts to place headphones in his ears.

EXHALE

"You need to stop acting like a child" Jane says.

He side eyes her and says "Screw you. You didn't even have to step in."

"Marcus, I was defending you." She tries to plead to him. But she hears his music get louder on his headphones so she gives up and stays silent during the rest of the train ride.

Walking back to the house, Marcus walks upstairs and slams his door which cause Jane to feel a little guilty for upsetting him.

She enters into her room and drops her bag on her bed, spreading her books and assignments out to see what else she has to do. She tries to complete some more assignments but her mind won't let her focus on anything other than her brother. So, she decides to reach into her drool for her Ziploc bag and walk towards his door.

She knocks, only to watch Marcus open it quickly and slam it in her face. She knocks back on his door again and whispers, "I have that nug if you want it."

She can hear his guitar playing from outside of the door, but it stops as he creaks the door open to hold his hand out. Jane chuckles as she slaps his hand away, pushing through the door.

"I thought this was a drop off thing." he says.

"It can be but I want to talk."

Jane sits on his bed and says, "We really haven't been spending much time together. I don't know if you ever did this before and I want to be the first if you haven't."

Marcus says, "What makes you think I haven't smoked before?" Reaching into his closet and pulling out a water pipe.

Jane says, "Well damn bro. We really haven't talked in a while. Well as I pack this device you have, tell me about your first time."

Marcus laughs as he hands her the bubbler. "Do you really want to know? Because it involves a lot of first times. First time with a man. First time with your friend."

"Neal?" Jane says. "You smoked with Neal before and he was your first?"

"Well he offered first and you always smoke in solitude." he says. "And yea, I always thought he was sweet. He's not really a jerk all of the time. He's just a colorful person."

Jane says, "Well it's good to know there's more than one side to that boy. I never offered because I thought it was irresponsible or you would rat. Your constant pettiness makes me question if I can trust you with my secrets."

"Even though I trust you with mine." Marcus says.

"Yea, I mean. I don't know. I guess you have a point."

Marcus watches her as she ponders away into her thoughts. "Hey, are you going to pack that or what?"

Jane packs the water pipe and passes it off to Marcus.

"Take the first hit. Let me see what I'm working with."

Marcus smirks and says confidently, "Hey, it's mine. I know how to hit it."

Jane stuffs a towel under the door and cracks open both of his windows. She sits down to watch her brother complete his hit, only to cough incessantly after.

Jane laughs as she turns his stereo on, combating his cough with music.

She says, "I thought you knew how to hit it."

Marcus, almost hacking up a lung says, "I do but that doesn't stop her from being a bitch."

The two of them smoke and listen to Marcus' indie rock music. As they converse about Neal and Marcus relationship.

"I'm not a stoner. I only smoke with Neal and sometimes Krishad."

"Who the hell is Krishad?" Jane asks.

"He's a friend. You wouldn't know him."

"So how often do you smoke with Neal?" Jane asks as she takes another hit.

He says, "Not often because he's usually high from smoking with you. I really love when we do. We really connect and I think that's special."

"Oh yea. I bet there's loads of connecting when you two get together."

"Jane, shut up. It's not even like that. Spiritually connect, not physically. You know how the herb brings people together."

Jane laughs and says, "Trust me, I know."

Marcus says, "I really do have to stop smoking with Krishad. His herb is weird and he likes to do other drugs."

"Have you done other stuff with him?" Jane asks.

"No, I've always been too chicken."

"Good." she says. "You should stay away from people like that. The urge to get higher can lead somewhere you don't want to go if not prepared."

"Yea, I feel you on that Jane. Maybe we can smoke together more."

Jane passes him the bubbler and says, "For sure. You ain't that bad little bro."

Marcus takes another hit as Jane leaves a nug on her dresser.

She looks at the time and starts to head into her room.

"I got to catch up on schoolwork so you finish that off."

Marcus nods his head and starts to take another hit. His eyes are barely open but they shine with happiness.

DAY 5

As Mr. Dimonte strolls in front of the class, he says, "Today's the last day for the oral assignment. Once everybody has read their work, I will collect and grade the remaining ones to hand it back to you next week."

"Note I will not grade for creativity." he says with a small glint in his eyes. "Just grammar and structure since it is difficult to grade one's perspective."

Mr. Dimonte shrugs his shoulders as he side eye's Jane a smug look, sitting back down in his chair as he speaks, "Who would like to begin today?"

Jane looks out at the class to see who's next to volunteer as she holds the satisfaction of hearing Mr. Dimonte's submit in her heart. And one by one, classmates stand up in front of the class to recite a variety of poetry, short stories and haikus, slightly sparking Jane's interest enough to let the class fly by.

Once class ends, Mr. Dimonte picks up all of the assignments from the bin before announcing the one for next week.

He says, "Next week's assignment is to write a continuation story to this sentence, 'When Stacey told Tracy to face me in the hallway, I told her....'".

Q. IMAGINE

"You can write it down or try to memorize it but it does need to be incorporated in your work."

And as Mr. Dimonte speaks over the crowd of students exiting his class, he says before the door slams shut and the once rambunctious sounds of eager teenagers comes to a hastily silence, "It doesn't necessarily have to rhyme, just go wherever your mind takes you. Be creative."

"I look forward to reading your assignments."

For lunch, the gang meets up at Uncle Sook's. Jane arrives last as everyone decides to meet up at the restaurant instead of at the back entrance of the school. She hears her friends in the ruby beaded room, walking in to see trays of food already on the table.

"Whoa. What's this?" she says

Neal speaks to her as he hands her a tray, "Uncle Sook hooked us up because I told him what happened yesterday. I wanted to apologize with food."

Jane smiles and she takes the tray from him, "I'm over it. I'm also sorry for slapping you."

Neal leans in to hug her as they embrace in healing old wounds and letting go of the past. Once Jane takes her tray and sits down near Lianne, Neal turns towards the rest of the group and says, "So what is everyone wearing tonight for the party?"

Lianne says, "I'm thinking about wearing a blue bikini with a grass luau skirt. Also thinking about rocking a flower."

"Oh, so you're trying to blend in with the basics tonight?" Neal says.

Lianne replies, "Well what are your suggestions Neal? There's not much you could wear to a luau."

Neal tilts his head and he ponders for a little bit. "How about you try a flower crown? One of those elegant Greek goddess-looking ones. Then find a really pretty tropical cover-up and tie that around her waist.

"Okay. Okay, that's not a bad idea.", Lianne says. "Wow Neal, you have vision. You might have to come to my house and help me with this."

"Text me." Neal replies.

The group convenes in laughter as Neal entertains the idea of being Lianne's personal stylist. Roscoe turns his attention towards getting the hookah ready for the group to smoke.

After the hose goes around the table and the coals eventually die out, the chatter silences as everyone's ears get attuned to the sounds flowing from the speakers. Roscoe recedes in his chair and watches the ruby beads swing side to side. Lianne and Neal enter into a trance as they rest their bodies on one another while Jane looks up towards the ceiling, envisioning tonight and the prospect of the party.

She drifts to the depths of her mind, becoming parallel between her dreamscape and reality, hearing Uncle Sook's music in the background but seeing flashes of light within an expansive space. She sees glimpses of the party, fading away like bubbles taken by the wind. She sees her outfit and her friends at Joe's house while feeling the energy of the party fill her heart.

A faint voice starts to appear in her ear, as her eyes begin to only see a mixture of colors.

All changes happen for a reason.

"Go away" she says.

You're going to need to know this.

"Jane" yells Lianne. As Jane opens her eyes.

"Who are you talking to?" Lianne asks, puzzled to hear her friend whisper to herself.

Surprised, Jane looks around the room to see if anyone heard her.

"I wasn't talking to anyone. I was thinking aloud."

"Well we only have 7 minutes left." Lianne says as she opens up her container.

Jane rubs her eyes trying to adjust to the sudden return to reality. She opens up her container as well and tries to finish her food before they have to go. While she's eating, she can't help but think about Alice coming back into her head again. She tries to keep her mind on the time and focus on finishing her food but she's so perplexed by the voice and the words that she can barely eat and ponder at once.

Walking back to the back gate of the school, bellies full and heads wandering the planes. Roscoe says, "So what is everybody drinking tonight?"

Lianne quickly says, "Joe is making punch so that's my drink for the night."

"No pregame?" asks Roscoe.

Jane laughs to herself and says, "Not everyone has a tolerance like you Roscoe. Not everyone can live, eat and breathe substances."

Roscoe rolls his eyes and laughs. "Of course, you say that Jane. You don't know how to loosen up."

Jane rolls her eyes. "Yes, I do. I know how to have fun and turn up."

"Yea, okay. Sometimes with weed but not on alcohol." he doubtedly says. "You sit there and watch people dance and have fun. That's your fun Jane. Watching."

The gang laughs while Jane blows off Roscoe's comments. Once they make it past the gate and put on their sunglasses, they start to head off in different directions for class.

Neal says, "So are we meeting at Joe's later?"

Lianne says "I think that's best. I don't know how long it's going to take me to get ready."

Jane agrees and says, "Same girl."

"Okay, so I guess we're all meeting at Joe's then" Neal says.

The group nods their head in agreement as they soon part ways and head to their last periods of class.

On the walk home, Jane thinks about the prospects of the night. Thinking of what scandals may go down for the last hoorah of summer and whether Tola is going to make an appearance there tonight.

When she gets home, she searches through her closet for the desired outfit of the night. But as she rummages through her closet, she hears a knock on her door.

"Come in." she says.

Marcus enters through the door and says, "So you heard about that beach party all the seniors are going to?"

Jane, with her back turned as she continued to search for her luau outfit, replies, "Yea. What about it?"

Marcus asks, "Are you going?"

Jane replies, "Obviously" before stumbling across her teal luau outfit, spotting it in one of the crevices of her closet.

Marcus says, "Cool. That means we can walk together to Joe's."

Jane laughs, "Marcus please. You know you weren't invited."

"Jane. I need to go. Neal's going and I want to work out things with him."

"Things like what?" She asks.

"Our relationship."

"Marcus, no. You're not going. You saw what happened yesterday and you don't even like to drink. Why would you even want to go?"

He says, "Jane, I need to go. I need you to have my back on this."

Jane looks at him and she sees his eyes filled with a desperate plea. She's determined not to babysit her brother tonight but can see the importance of reconciling him with Neal.

She sits on her bed and says, "How about you just ask him to come over after? Trust me, you don't want to see Neal at the party, it's just going to make you feel more insecure."

Upon hearing her last sentence, Marcus looks away to hold back the tears.

Jane tries to cheer him up by saying, "Maybe that's why you should call him before. You never know, if your offer's good enough, he may change his mind and come straight here."

Marcus looks back at her and smiles. "Yea, let me get on that."

"Yea, no pun intended" Jane replies.

"Good. So now that we've solved that problem, I need you to leave because... I'm still going to the party."

As she nudges him out of the door, he says "The party thing wasn't off of the table yet."

"It was never on the table."

Jane walks downstairs in her luau halter top and mini skirt, with her wristlet in hand and her eyes on a promising night. She thinks to herself, "You are fine as hell", while she strolls past her parents in the dining room and heads towards the front door.

"Whoa. Whoa. Where do you think you're going?" Jane hears from the dining room.

She paces back and says, "One of my friends is having a party at his house. I was on my way there."

Isaac stands up and walks towards Jane, as his eyes widen when he sees the length of her clothing.

"And why do you think it's a good idea to go alone to this party? Especially in the middle of the night and dressed in a limited amount of clothing." he asks.

"Go back upstairs. I'm not letting you go to this party."

Isaac walks back into the dining room as Jane runs to him and pleads, "Dad, it's only 7:30. All of my friends are already there and it's not far from the house. Joe is someone I'm graduating with and someone who has been in my classes since the 5th grade."

Isaac says, "Okay, but you would still walk by yourself to the party. Not to mention the walk back home, which would be a later time.

Jane quickly says, "What if I bring Marcus to the party?"

Isaac and Billie look at each other as they ponder on Jane's request.

Billie looks at her and says, "I think that will be fine. Just make sure you two stick together."

Jane smiles as she gets the O.K. to go, but soon regrets even bringing it up since now he has to tag along. She walks back up the stairs and quickly opens Marcus' door, saying "You got your wish. You can come to the party with me."

Marcus jumps out of his bed and almost drops his phone, quickly closing the door to get ready as Jane tells him to hurry up.

They both head out of the door after agreeing with their father on the time, stepping into the chilly night and walking along the dimly lit sidewalk. She looks into the night, preparing for the fun of hanging out with her friends. She looks at Marcus as he sees the same grin plastered onto his face as they both fight the wind.

"Whoa, it's chilly. Maybe I should have worn a heavier coat."

Marcus says, "Don't worry. The walk home won't be that bad. Plus, you look really nice."

Jane says, "Thank you. The walk home is never an issue, especially with all of the alcohol Joe told us he was having."

As Jane and Marcus turn the corner, they begin to hear the loud bass of a stereo tremble in Joe's house. The crowds of teens standing outside on the sidewalk make it hard for Jane and Marcus to get close to the house. But as she passes through, she looks into the crowds to see if any of them are her friends. She tells Marcus to look around for them as she begins to hear what sounds like her friends. Until she hears from Jane, "Okay Jane. I see the fleekness. Too cool to walk in with us now."

Jane looks around until her eyes meet Roscoe's face as she walks towards him and sees the other two next to him.

"Looking for someone?" Neal says to Jane, holding a drink in his hand. He takes a sip as he realizes Marcus is standing right next to her, pulling his cup from his lip. He chokes a little.

Jane says, "Yea guys, extra member of the group tonight. Although there may be another one since Tola said that he'd might be coming."

Neal tries to recover as he says "I didn't see him yet. He's not the type to party anyway so he may not be coming."

Jane says "Yea maybe. I'll text him to see if he's really coming."

Jane pulls out her phone to text Tola, while everyone heads into the party. Neal leads the way as they enter through the door and try to bypass the crowded hallway.

The reddish tint from the living room lights give the room an alluring feel. The couples dancing to the rap music blasting out only intensifies the allure and the thrill of the night. Jane, Lianne and Roscoe grab a cup and fill it up with punch while Marcus glances around to check out who else is at the party.

Neal finishes his cup before approaching Marcus to talk, only to be rejected as Marcus walks away from him. Neal turns his frustration towards his cup and refills it to the rim, only to spill it as he tries to chug whatever stays in the cup. He hastily walks into the kitchen area of the house, prompting the rest of them to follow.

Lianne sees Joe with all of this friends, playing cards. Joe spots them as they enter and gets up to greet. "Glad you beautiful ladies could make it, including you Neal and Roscoe."

Roscoe says, "Thank you. I know my dreads can be deceiving."

Joe laughs, "Do you guys want to play horse races?"

Neal declines as Lianne says, "How do you play?"

"It's easy. I'll show you." Joe says as he sets up the game.

"You just place bets on a suit, like spades, diamonds, clubs and hearts. You flip the cards on the deck and each card that had your suite moves the card in play, forward. The one who reaches the top wins."

Jane says, "That's sounds fun."

Joe says, "Cool. There's still room for this round if you want to jump in now?"

They both sit down to play while Neal and Roscoe watch from afar.

Jane yells to Roscoe. "Now who's watching the fun." As Roscoe raises his cup in a humble submit.

Joe says, "Who do you guys want to bet on?"

Jane says, "I bet on hearts", while everyone else at the tables yells out their bets.

Joe and his friends place the bets and Joe initiates the game. "On your mark! Get set! Go!", he yells as he begins to flip the cards.

Diamonds and Clubs are up and so far, spades and hearts haven't left the stables. Then suddenly hearts is up and it's just spades. Jane, still confident in her suite, cheers it on. Spades starts to move and catches to where clubs is, right behind diamonds. Lianne starts to panic because her suit is not last. Joe flips another card and its spades! Spades is now head to head for the winning ticket. Joe intensifies the anticipation.

"Okay ladies and gents, this is the final card. Will it be spades? Or will it be diamonds?" he says.

Jane feeling the punch, yells out "Spades!"

Joe then flips up the card and before he puts it down. He looks around and wickedly smiles at everyone that's playing.

"Put it down already!" Lianne yells.

He slams the card down and yells, "Spades!"

Jane stands up from her chair and dances in joy of winning. She then says, "Drink up now", bragging about her win.

The group looks at her and as Lianne says, "I thought you placed your bet on hearts."

Jane looks puzzled as she remembers her bet. Her sudden looks of shock prompts her group of friends to burst out into laughter.

They all yell out, "Drink" as Jane side eyes her friends while taking a sip.

Joe walks towards her and says, "Take another one for your mistake."

Everyone drinks and Joe asks the girls for another round in which they both agree.

Jane looks back and still sees Neal and Roscoe standing around and watching. She sees Marcus enter into the room which calms her since she forgot he was here.

Jane tries to wave Neal and Roscoe over to play but they both shake their heads no and agree to just watch. They post up on the far wall of the kitchen until Neal walks off with Marcus and

Roscoe walks back into the living room.

Jane bet to 4 sips on spades. Lianne moves to diamonds and everyone else places their bets. The game begins and spades is up again by two cards. Jane feels the luck and starts to cheer on her suit. The next three cards are hearts. Jane holds face, still believing in her suit. Joe flips the card and its, clubs. He flips and flips, and every other suit advances except spades.

Finally, it's time for the last card draw and it's between hearts and clubs. Joe intensifies the game again by hyping up the anticipation. The card he throws down is clubs. Jane and Lianne both look at each other, saddened by both of their cards not winning. They listen to Joe's friend bet and he bets half a cup on clubs along with his other friend betting half a cup on clubs. Joe looks at both of the girls and says, "You ladies might need to refill your cup."

Lianne says, "I'm good. I still have a half cup left."

Joe says, "Yeah that's not enough. They both bet half a cup on clubs so that means you need to drink both of their bets, which is a whole cup."

Jane and Lianne's mouths drop in shock. Jane re iterates to clarify. "So, we have to chug a cup of punch?" she asks.

Joe smiles at them and nods his head.

The two girls then walk back to the punch bowl and refill their cups. They then walk back to the table and proceed to chugging their cup along with everyone else at the table who also lost.

After drinking half, they both gasp for air and then try to dust off the other half. When finished, they gasp again in reprieve, slowly sitting down and awaiting Joe to start round three.

Joe laughs as he sees the two girls feel the effects of chugging the punch. "Why don't you guys take a break? I have to check on the rest of the party and we can play some beer pong later."

Lianne looks up at Joe, holding her hand out so he can help her up. She says, "Yea, I'll walk with you. I kind of want to see the rest of the party too."

They both head into the living room as Lianne flashes Jane a smile. Jane laughs and winks back as she already knows the mischief behind her antics. But while Jane remains seated, she really starts to feel the buzz from the alcohol. Her head starts to throb from all the noises at the party, stemming from her classmates shouting and dancing, to the music blasting and shaking the house. Everything overwhelms her and she gets weak at the knees when she tries to stand. But to her relief, Marcus is near to catch her before she falls.

"You okay party girl?" Marcus says to Jane.

Jane says as she tries to brush it off, "Yea, I'm fine. That punch hit me all at once but I'm okay. Just got a little light headed."

"Okay. Maybe we should get some air."

Jane agrees as Marcus moves out of the way, though as he steps backwards, he runs into one of Joe's teammates. The teammate shoves him as he's walking into the kitchen, forcing him to collapse into Jane and knock her off balance.

"Whoa athlete! Someone's a little aggressive." Neal says as he tries to help the both of them up.

"Shut up Neal! No one asked for your opinion."

"Maybe you shouldn't shove my boyfriend out of the way. Then I wouldn't give my opinion, Aaron."

"Don't start with me, panzy." Aaron says as his grip on the cup gets tighter.

"What did you just call me?" Neal replies, as he steps closer to him.

Aaron walks closer and tries to shove Neal across the room. But before Aaron could slash another comeback at him, Neal hauls into him and knocks him and Joe's kitchen table over. He flails his fists into his face as Aaron tries to swing him off of him as well as get some hits in.

But the fight quickly dissolves as Joe flies into the kitchen and grabs Neal off of Aaron, while the other football players try to hold Aaron back.

"I'm going to kill him!" Aaron screams in a fury, trying his best to get free from his teammates. But Joe shoves Neal across the kitchen and fiercely stares into Aaron's eyes, glaring back at them as he checks the damage done to his kitchen table. One of the legs broke off which only ignites his anger.

"What the hell is wrong with you?! This is how you both treat my house! Get out!" he screams. Lianne tries to console him.

"Joe, wait. They didn't mean it."

"No. I'm not having this in my house! My mom is coming home in a few days and now I have to fix this."

Aaron jumps in and says, "Hey man, I can fix this for you tomorrow."

Joe looks at him with disgust and says, "I told you to get out!"

"C'mon man."

In an instance, Joe runs over to Aaron and forcefully tries to shove him out. He grabs Neal as Marcus, Jane and Lianne follow. Once Joe gets to the door after pushing through the crowd of people, he shove both Neal and Aaron out as Jane and Marcus start to plead.

"Joe, c'mon. Let's not drag this out of hand. I mean, Neal is your friend..."

"Yea I know, but I'm not going to tolerate people who can't handle their liquor. Especially when it comes to disrespecting my house."

Lianne says to Joe, "Okay. Let's cool off. Let's rethink this, maybe those two just need some air."

Lianne walks him upstairs to calm him down while Jane turns to Neal to see if he's okay.

"Neal, what happened? I mean...I didn't even see how it all began."

Neal looks away as he shakes his head and starts to walk down the block to cool off. "I need a moment. I just need to rethink my life right now."

"Neal, wait!" Marcus yells as he follows him. Neal changes from walking to sprinting to get away.

As Neal yells, "No. Just give me space."

Jane watches them both run away into the mystique of the

night, feeling the cool breeze of the brush across her face as it calms her as much as it soothes her. The buzzing of her phone in her bag takes her away from the relaxing moment as she sees a text from Tola saying 'Can't make it tonight. Call me when you're done.'

Jane says aloud in frustration, "Why? So, we can go for another walk? Or is this the night you make your move because you think I'm drunk enough to fall for it?"

She sits down on the stoop, deciding whether she should leave or try and find her friends. But then she remembered her pact with her father which ultimately determines her decision. She walks in the direction of where Neal and Marcus ran off in order to find them and see if they want to stay at the party or not.

Though as she gets up from sitting on the stoop, she feels the sway of the alcohol hit her again as it knocks her off balance.

She stumbles down the block from Joe's as she starts yelling out for them.

"Neal! Enough cooling off already. It's time to go back. Marcus, it's time to go."

She walks and turns down every block she thinks they took.

She's unaware of where they are and where she is going.

She hears a voice say, "Excuse me" in a very low tone. Jane quickly looks around to see where it came from.

After several minutes of searching, she turns back to find her way to Joe's house, feeling her drunken state intensify the more she walks on.

She walks past a group of people sitting on the stairs, listening to the music inside and noting how similar it is to the music Joe was playing.

She hears a voice say at the house, "Your friend is in here." The voice is much deeper than anyone she knows but she thinks it's just one of Joe's football friends that goes to another school. Jane looks into the house as she walks up the stairs, thinking the house is Joe's until one of the guys behind her says, "Where are you going?"

Jane looks back at the man smiling at her. His handsome grin takes her mind back to the incident she had on her walk home from school, as well as the man on the train. She notices the same demeanor he had after their shoulders collided, even though his appearance didn't look as mystique without his all black suit on.

"Do you remember me Jane?"

She says, "How do you know my name?"

He says as he walks up the stairs, "I remember you. I see you didn't take my advice."

"You're still spacing out to your surroundings, walking into people's homes you don't know."

Jane tries to quickly walk down the stairs. She says, "Excuse me. I need to leave. My friends are waiting for me.

The strange man blocks her from leaving with his arm. He pushes himself against her and looks deeply into her eyes. He says, "Wait. I'm just joking. There's no rush to leave. You know I have my eye on you."

"Just relax. You'll be okay. Just relax."

Jane begins to shake as the buzz from the punch begins to leave. She says, "I don't want anything you have. I want to leave."

The man brings her closer and rubs her head. Jane is paralyzed in fear. He says, "Shh. Why are you so afraid? You think I would hurt my prize possession."

"C'mon. Just hang out for a moment. I got some good stuff for you. Some weed. Some drinks, some food and love. Just sit down and relax."

Jane walks closer to the mysterious man as he takes her hand and sits her down on the stairs. He pulls out a blunt and starts to light it to calm her down.

"Jane, my name is Sonny. I'm a really big fan of you."

Sonny passes the blunt to Jane. Jane takes it with tears in her eyes as she holds it in her hand.

He says, "Why don't you relax?"

He rubs her arm on her shoulder and she flinches.

"Relax. Just relax. You're in my care now. No one is going to hurt you."

Jane looks into the house and sees some girls around her age in the house. She sees older men sitting by them as the girl's faces are hidden by their hair.

Sonny says, "You know Jane. I really admire who you are. How strong you are with your friends and how you keep that young boy in check. What's his name again? Tola?"

Q. IMAGINE

Jane begins to cry as she mutters, "Please. Please let me go."

Sonny gets angry and says in a harsher tone. "You know that's what's wrong with you spoiled rich kids. Nothing is ever enough for you. Now I said hit the blunt, now hit it!"

His loud tone brings Jane into a panic as she tries to smoke the blunt but it falls from her hand.

Sonny tries to pick it up and as he leans, Jane tries to run off of the stoop.

He quickly grabs her and brings her close to him. Jane sobs woefully and pleads, "Please, let me go."

"I know you like to smoke. Why? Why are you acting this way with me Jane? Do you know all that I've done to be close to you. Do you know I made this party just for you?"

"Do you?!" Sonny yells as she shakes Jane in his arms. She cries and pleads again as Sonny begins to kiss her cheek and neck.

In a soft whisper, Jane pleads "Just let me go. You don't know my family."

"Oh, I don't know your family?" Sonny yells. "You don't know who I know?"

Sonny laughs and smiles from ear to ear.

He throws her on the stoop and says again, "You don't know who I know."

Jane looks into her bag for her phone but the moment she looks up, she sees Sonny pointing a gun in her face.

His tone changes as he says, "Don't try to be smart now? You press a button on the phone, it might be the last thing you see."

"You've truly got some attitude girl. But I like that. It's fun."

Sonny walks off of the stoop with his gun in hand and says, "Man I have plans for you."

Jane holds her phone, hesitantly as Sonny points the gun at her again. Though her eyes light up when she sees Neal and Marcus walking down the block.

Jane cries, "Marcus!"

Sonny quickly looks behind him and slides his gun away. As Neal and Marcus walk towards them, suspicious of what is going on as they see Jane with tears in her eyes.

"Jane." Neal says. "Are you okay? What are you doing?"

Sonny stares at Neal and Marcus as he tries to soften his grip on Jane. He looks into the house to signal his henchman to come outside. As he places a fake smile on his face and says, "She's fine man. We're friends and we're just getting to know each other a little better."

"Jane", Marcus hesitantly says.

Jane pleads, "Don't leave. I'm ready to go back to the party."

Though as Jane tries to stand up, Sonny walks over to her and puts his arm around her.

He glares at them intently and says, "She'll meet you there. We're almost done rekindling."

Neal says firmly, "You need to let go of her" as he whispers to Marcus to call the cops.

Marcus waits behind him and secretly tries to call 9-1-1. Though the moment Marcus dials the number, one of his henchman clears his throat and reveals his pistol.

As Neal and Marcus' eyes widen.

"Jane, get up." Sonny says.

"Tell your friends you'll meet them at the party a little later."

"I can't." she pleads as she tries to wiggle free from his grasp. Sonny gives her a deathly stare and says, "You can and you will."

Neal can see the fear held in Jane's eyes while watching Sonny and his henchmen dauntingly stare them down.

Neal bravely says, "We're not leaving without her." and steps up the stairs to reach out his hand to her.

One of his henchman moves behind him and separates Neal from Marcus.

Jane leans forward to reach for Neal's hand nervously. She sees the beautiful glint in his eye as he reaches out to help. She doesn't see one of the men pull out a gun and point it directly at Neal's head. Though with the sound that shattered Jane's image of Neal, she saw and re-lived the friendship that blossomed from the moment they met in 8th grade.

She remembers the first time she saw that beautiful glint in his eyes, though with that first impression came this lasting image, splattered all over her in ways she did not know.

Jane yells out as she feels her body being whisked away, "Neal! Neal!" As she hears Marcus' scream diminish a few moments before another gunshot sounds off.

CHAPTER I

Jane wakes up to feel her body limp, her wrists clenched in metal chains as her feet dangle on the cold metal floor. She can feel her head pounding as if someone was punching her from within her skull but the agony becomes worse when she tries to soothe the pain.

She tries to reach for her head to massage the pain but when she reaches up, her arms are restricted and bound. A sudden shriek of fear shoots up her spine when she realizes she has no idea where she is.

Why is she here?

And how she came to be in this position?

For a few minutes she tries to grab landing on the soles of her feet but her legs wobble and collapse at the attempt to truly stand. The fatigue and disorient from the previous night takes a hold of her body as she tries to stand and land on solid ground. She tries to grab a hold of reality. Her vision clears but the sight she sees, or the lack of sight muddles her to her core. Her eyes are open yet she can only see a vast pitch of darkness.

She tries to wake up from this elaborate lucid dream but the crown of her head brings her to a state of distress.

"This pain is real. This is all real. This isn't a dream."

As panic starts to set in as she can only move her legs and feet. She tries to yank her wrist from the chains, squeezing and folding her hands through so she can escape. The cold metal shackles doesn't budge. There is no leeway in the chains and the friction of trying to escape makes her bleed. The blood drips down her arm as she keeps trying, her heart start to race as there's no budge in the chains. Her mind wanders.

"Where am I?"

The grimmest thoughts start to plague her mind as the fear takes a hold of her and tries to control her body She stares into the darkness and drifts into her mind wondering how she is going to escape this. And what will happen if she can't.

Jane screams and wails trying to gain someone's attention, hoping someone will release her and free her from this trap she's in. Her one glance of hope is diminished as she looks around and sees nothing in this opaque chamber.

She fears her capture is the only person who can hear her or find her. The one sole being who knows she is in this hell. She squints her eyes to grasp any object of light that could be a tool to her salvation. She sees nothing. No shimmer of reprieve. No glimpse of life. Nothing.

"What is this?" she says wistfully.

Her eyes bleed of cries as she remembers what she saw that night. Neal and her brother start to concern her mind. She tries to shake off the doubt in order to keep faith alive but her confidence is no match for the inevitable outcome she fears she must face. She bows her head to the defeat of time, knowing that sooner or later she will face the reasons of her captivity.

Q. IMAGINE

"How am I going to get out of this?" Jane pleads.

As she hears a voice.

Don't give up Jane. Don't give up.

"Alice!" she cries out. "What am I doing here?" Her words are engulfed in agony and fear.

Believe in your wit Jane. All is to come and reveal itself. Don't give up.

"Help me! Help me get out of here!" she pleads.

Though her cries of agony become silenced as she hears a stir within the pitch-black chamber. As Alice's voice silences, the sound of footsteps increase and head in her direction.

As Jane sees a tall, large figure walking towards her. She feels fear start to settle into her heart as the powerful steps of a man is heard and the sound of his breath become known to her ears.

She feels the brawn and powerful footsteps shake the chains and floor as the final steps come to a halt. Only a few feet in front of her does this man stand where she hangs. His face is revealed to her when the sound of a light flickers on and illuminates a portion of this opaque chamber. Her eyes flinch at the flick of a light. One they focus, she sees the image of eyes gleaming within slits of a ski mask.

She is mystified to see a greasy large man with his shirt and arms stained with blood and grime. The dirt and sweat covering his arms and neck sent a cringe down Jane's spine. As she looks upon his grotesque figure. A grotesque man lifts up the bottom of his ski mask and reveals his large encrusted lips and malevolent smile. He walks closer to her, forcing her to breath in the stench from his mouth. The spit flinging onto her face with each word he dares to speak.

"Look at me."

The smell of his breath turns her stomach ill. She looks down because she can't bare the stench this man spews as his creepy smile grips her heart.

"Look at me girl." he says, holding her face still while she tries to turn from his gaze.

"Don't be shy. Boss told me not to lay a hand on you but you will listen to me when I tell you to do something."

She can see his smile turn darker as he slides his hands up her dress and touches her thigh. He stretches his greasy hands up and down her dress as the more he pushes himself closer, the more Jane tries to recede from him.

He brings her closer to him and says, "But boss isn't here right now. So do not provoke me girl. I don't need much to try and have some fun with you."

He slowly removes his hand and walks back towards the light, pulling out a chair from the now illuminated desk. He sits in silence as he watches her a few feet ahead.

Jane doesn't move a muscle in order to keep the man away from her. She looks around and tries to catch a glimpse of a means to an escape.

Jane can feel his eyes creep over her body and analyze her figure hidden under her dress. And as she hears the sinister chuckles from across the room, she continues to look to find a way to escape this captivity.

She sees no entrance way nor windows but she knows that there has to be something beyond the shadows to lead to her escape. How else would she and this man be in this room without a way in and a way out?

Jane starts to play a daring idea in her mind. An idea of provoking him starts to dance around in the fantasy of getting free.

She thinks that if he loosens the chains, she could have a moment to escape this place. Her mind juggles between getting free and creating more danger but she sees this as the only opportunity to survive and relinquish herself from these chains.

Jane begins to furiously shake the metal chains and wail so loud the echoes bounce off of the walls. The man willfully steps out of the chair and walks towards her. The weight of his body lifting up causes the chair to push back and fall to the ground.

He looks at her with the most cynical intent gleaming in his eyes, walking towards her furiously and pushing his greasy body close to hers.

He gazes his eyes on every aspect of her body once he feels her warmth pushed up against him. Jane fights the repulsive tinge that shoots up and down her body as this man ogles her from every angle he can glance at. He brushed his hand across her face as she winces by the subtle chill in his touch. He smiles and starts to look deep into her eyes, slipping his hand under her dress and relishing on the sensation of her skin.

Jane jerks her body to remove his hands from her. She jerks so hard that her wrist start to throb and sear in pain.

He moves his face close to hers and makes their lips touch. He says "I warned you about this. Is this not what you want?"

Jane jerks in her chains to try anything to get herself away from him. She feels the fear set back in as her plan has backfired. As she dreads the next moments of her life if she cannot get free.

He walks behind her and lifts both hands under her dress and under her panties.

"I told you what would happen if you were to make noise." he grimly says.

Jane jerks her body again as her heart beats furiously. Her heart beats so fast she can barely catch a breath as she jerks to get free. He walks back towards the front of her and forcefully spreads her legs open with one hand.

"Now you're going to make a lot of noise. Because I want you to."

He removes his hand from her panties and unbuckled his pants and zip them down.

Trembling in fear, she quickly crosses her legs and uses the weight of the chains to swing her legs behind her. She looks up and prays for something to happen. Something to stop this man from doing what he has in store.

He pulls his pants down to expose his sizeable length as he gets ready to take what he wants from her, but in this grim moment before the deed is done, Jane hears Alice.

Don't give up Jane.

Jane starts to shake her head in disbelief. Any strength she had was diminished when her plan failed. This man starts to move closer to her as he strokes himself and watches her suffer in this dreadful moment.

"Don't worry sweetie. You might enjoy this." His cynicism makes her skin crawl as she holds her legs closer together. Gripping them so tight, her muscles starts to lock together.

Jane hears Alice say "fight", but she feels no fight left in her.

He steps towards her to grab her waist closer to his hands. He starts to lift up her dress and squeeze himself between her clenching legs.

Jane begins to weep as she shakes and clenches her legs close for dear life.

Alice comes back.

Fight Jane. This is the moment. Do not give up. Fight now

He whispers to her, "Open your legs girl. Don't make me get rough."

Fight now.

"You don't want me to get rough?"

Fight.

In an instance, Jane starts to swing her body again to loosen her grip as the man tries to pry open her legs. She swings her legs back to force the man to lose his grip. And in the moment, she launches her knees forward and punts him forward onto the ground as he keels over in agony.

His laughter and smile of joy turns to screams as he clenches himself on the floor. His eyes clench shut as he wishes the pain away. As Jane tries to loosen her wrists within the chains to get free.

He looks up at Jane with pure rage in his eyes. He stares passionately into them as her eyes stare back at him with a fearless intent. Her strength builds as the adrenaline surges through her body preparing for an escape.

"You're going to regret that." he yells in agony.

The disadvantage sets in as she hasn't found a way out of these chains blocking her from her freedom. Though instead of letting doubt plague her, she sets it in her mind that she will get free. She's determined to prevent this perverse man. This instrument of fear trying to take advantage of her. Her tenacity to fight encompasses any idea of doubt or fear in her mind.

The man struggles to get to his feet as he continues to hold his throbbing genitals in his hand. He tries to stand up but fails as he falls back to his knees and inches in pain.

Revenge is cut short when the large metal door in the distance swings wide open and illuminates Jane's chamber, revealing it to be an old storage container.

The door swings wide open as Jane starts to hear the sounds of waves splashing and feel the sun shine on her and the chains. She starts to notice the group of men entering the container and witnessing the large man on his eyes while Jane remaining in her bloody chains.

To her surprise, she recognizes the faces of the men walking in. Although they look slightly different in the light than how they did the night of Joe's party. She sees the slick smile of Sonny as he rubs his hand across her chin and her lips.

In anger, she shakes her chains and yells at them, "Let me the fuck out! I didn't do anything to you!"

The man whom she befriended says, "You didn't have to. Your beauty was enough for me."

He pulls out a sandwich from his pocket and begins to take a few bites out of it. He gazes his eyes all over her body as he did when they first met.

"You've really got some fire in you girl. I saw that a week ago, and last night."

His calm demeanor sickens her and ignites a fury in her eyes. She stares at him in disgust. He takes another bite of the sandwich before shoving the rest in her face. He tauntingly saying, "Take a bite Jane. I know you're hungry."

Jane briskly turns her face as he keeps trying to shove it between her lips.

"You need to eat girl. I got to keep you strong." His eyes widening as if he's trying to hypnotize her to listen.

His scheme starts to work as Jane moves her head towards the sandwich and grabs it within her teeth. His success is only diminished when she yanks it out of his hand and flails it across the shipping container.

The crew laughs in amusement, although stunned by how Jane

is reacting.

"We have a lively one here." one shouts in the distance.

Sonny is taken back but watches her as she insinuates with hatred for him in this fatal stare she holds. She jerks her body so hard towards him that she hears a snap and feels a break in both wrists. Jane starts to lose all sense to act rational and flails her body in her chains, doing anything possible to escape this captivity.

"Let me the hell out of these chains!" she yells. Jane jerks in the chains, feeling the crackling of bones shift under her skin. One of the crew members walks over to his boss but he pushes him away and watches Jane yell at the top of her lungs.

"I'm not doing anything you want me to! Let... Me. Go!" she yells.

Jane furiously screams and tries to pull her wrist out of the metal chains. She starts to feel the metal chains slide as a sharp pain shoots down her arms causing her to scream even louder.

She gets the chains to slide over the palms of her hands when she feels Sonny's hands around her neck. He lunges for her and tries to squeeze her unconsciously. Jane tries to break free of his grasp but her wrists still shackled makes it impossible to stop this man from choking her. She tries to gasp for air and stomp on his foot to loosen his grip. She lands one blow on his toe to break free from his grasp and catch a breath.

As Sonny yells, "Damnit!"

And in a last attempt to get free, she drops all of her weight to the floor and forces herself out of the chains. Jane regains her energy back before the crew start to close in and she dashes towards the door for her escape. But just when hope starts to prevail the boss grabs a hold of her hair and yanks her back. The chunks of hair start to pull out of her skull as he pulls her back to him. Jane bellows in pain as she fights his grip by trying to kick him. The other men start to close in on her as Jane starts to feel her chances of her escaping narrow down. She lets out one more kick and lands one right on his chest. As she pushes him backwards and releases her hair from his grasp.

Run Jane. Now's your chance.

Jane sees the crew closing in and sprints to the left to dodge their grasps. She then sprints in between the men closing in on her and out of the door.

"Don't let her escape." Jane hears from behind her. But Jane's feet and legs stay strong and keep moving forward as she feels the freedom she has hoped for.

At last.

Her adrenaline is radiating through her muscles as she reaches the cold air of the loading dock. She still hears the impending footsteps behind her, keeping her pushing on towards safety.

"Almost there." Jane thinks.

"I have to get home."

Her mind and body want to rest but her instinct is telling her to keep running. The fear of going back motivates her to keep pushing.

Alice starts to speak to her again as she peddles her feet down the loading dock and away from the henchman.

Let go Jane, I've got it from here.

"I have to get home", she thinks. Her mind starts to flash images of her family as the thought of reaching home fills her heart with bliss. Her legs become almost machine like as she keeps running. She refuses to stop until she sees her destination.

"I need to get home Alice!" she says aloud.

Trust me Jane. Stop running.

Jane ignores her and keeps running. She runs as fast as her legs can move.

She runs and runs until she feels boundless and free. As Jane floats off of the ground and into the air.

Her body still jerks as if she's on land yet she feels no mass. There is no floor beneath her and nothing surrounding her but air and water.

She looks down and sees the algae green water moving towards her at an increasing rate. Her eyes close as her body slaps into the water, knocking her unconscious.

Every particle of her body becomes numb to the freezing temperatures of the Hudson River. She drifts to the depths of the river, floating down into the abyss and out of sight from view.

She's not home but in her mind, she feels a sensation of tranquility. An indescribable feeling of nothing around her or within her.

No emotions. No water. Not even the weight of her own body.

She feels the voice of Alice as any thought in her mind starts to fade. Any fabric of this world start to drift into the null. She hears in her mind before she is completely undertaken to the other side.

Jane.

CHAPTER II

Surround yourself in nothing and you will find the answers to everything.

If nothing is close enough to sidetrack you, then nothing will limit you.

Your thoughts... endless.

Your potential...unlimited.

Beep

Beep

Beep

"Vitals are steady." the doctor says.

"Why hasn't she woken up?" asks Billie. She hovers over her daughter's comatose body, desperate to hear why her daughter isn't waking up. She stares into the doctor's eyes as she listens to every words he says.

"Unfortunately, ma'am, I don't have an answer for that. Severe mental traumas along with hypoxia can affect the brain and tissue causing a comatose state. Only time will tell when she wakes up. Just know your daughter is stable at the moment and there is hope for recovery."

"What do you mean 'time will tell'?" Billie asks as tears start to fall. "How much time will she stay in this?! We can't get anything definitive?"

The doctor shrugs his shoulders and says, "I'm sorry ma'am but that's as much as we know right now. All we can do is monitor her and make sure she stays stable."

Billie drops to her knees as she feels the weight of the news drag her to the floor. The doctor's words and the image of her daughter's still body ring through her mind as the woes of a hysterical mother flows throughout the hospital hallways. Her torment and despair overwhelms Isaac as he tries to console his wife. He lifts Billie off of the floor and tries to place her in the chair next to Jane's bed. But Billie flies to her daughter's side and grips her hand tightly. She rests her head on Jane's arm and prays. Prays for a miracle. Prays for her daughter to know she's safe.

"Lord I know it's been awhile since we spoke. I know I am undeserving to ask for your help since we don't talk. But if you give me one chance to prove myself. Please! Please bring my daughter back to me!"

She leans over and kisses her daughter on the forehead as tears flow onto Jane.

Billie releases every built-up emotion in her body. She sobs next to Jane and rests her head onto her chest. Isaac, unable to bear the sight of his distraught wife and comatose daughter, quickly tries to lift Billie off of Jane and console his wife outside of the room.

Marcus sits quietly in the corner of the room as he stares woefully at his older sister. He stands up and walks towards her bed, noticing the vibrant glow she always held in her face replaced with a dull and lifeless complexion. Her lips lost their bright pink color and held a greyish tint to them. Her normally slick curly locks were hidden in a wild mane of matted hair.

He leans next to his sister and kisses her on her cheek, pleading her to wake up. "Stay with us Jane. Please! Please wake up!"

Where do you go when you go to sleep?

Is it the same place you go when you have no place to stay?

Do you just wander?

Do you just wander around?

Floating through space until you find a place to stop.

But that kind of makes you think. Is there ever really a "stay"?

Is "stop" a natural occurrence if things are moving?

Always changing.

A distant faint noise becomes present to Jane's ears, enough to awaken her but too low to focus on.

Q. IMAGINE

Her eyes open.

As she feels the weight of her body but nothing else in sight. She sees nothing but the white space which makes her question whether her eyes are open or closed. And just to check, Jane tries to blink but the feeling of her eyelids doesn't present itself. She tries not to panic as she closes her eyes tightly and waits for that moment to awaken from this.

She waits for that moment and waits for a period of time. Until she loses track of time and opens them to see.

Nothing's changed.

Jane only sees a vastness of white space and nothing else.

No objects.

No sky.

No roof or floor.

She hears nothing but the sound of her breath and a faint sound in the distance that she can't make out. She looks around and tries to find any object.

But sees nothing and hears nothing.

Until Alice speaks.

This is what I was talking about Jane.

Jane looks around, hearing the whispering voice turn into a trembling force. It echoes through this blank space and send lights around this vast space.

I told you you're going to need this.

Jane tries to answer her but nothing comes out. She starts to panic as she tries to let out any sound possible.

Speak with your mind. Talk as if you're having a thought.

She tries to calm down after listening to Alice and asks in her mind, "Where am I?"

There you go...

"What is this place?"

Where are you? You are nowhere. What is this? This is everything and nothing at all.

"Where am I? Am I dead?"

You ask questions and expect the answers right away. Where are you? You are nowhere. Are you dead? Only if you believe you are.

"I don't understand!" Jane says as her patience runs thin.

The only way to understand is to think.

"Alice please!" Jane begs. "Help me!"

I am helping. What do you think I'm doing? But you have to do the work. I only assist.

"Okay. Okay, I'm listening. I will do what you ask and listen to what you say." Jane pleads.

How do I get home?"

Q. IMAGINE

What is home for you?

Jane plays along "America. New York. My family and friends. Everything I've known so far in my life!"

If that is home for you, then you have 3 of those 4 things right now.

"What?!"

Look around, what do you see? Do you see anything?

"NO!", Jane says angrily.

What are you thinking about?

"I'm thinking I want to get out of here!"

What is 'here' if you see nothing around you?

Jane starts to become overwhelmingly frustrated and confused. She tries to calm herself down and really think about what Alice is trying to convey.

"Where is here if you see nothing around you? Alice, I don't understand. And it doesn't matter where 'here' is because 'here' is the place I want to leave!

Jane, think about it. If there is nothing around you here. Nothing in your line of sight than how are you going to go somewhere else?

"Well maybe that's something you can help me with. All knowing." Jane says as she begins to rub her head.

If there is nothing here and nowhere to go. Then how do you know this isn't everything? Or where you want to be?

"Because I know there is somewhere else out of here, obviously. I wouldn't be trying to leave if I didn't know there wasn't something outside of 'here'. Wherever and whatever 'here' is. I wouldn't know anything other than what is here if this was the only place that existed. And why would I stay here? How is this even everything when there is nothing?"

Maybe that's something you should ask yourself. Where can there be a place where nothing exists and nothing is everything you see? And where is this place? Is it parallel to the places you know?

"Where can there be a place where there is nothing and everything? Where there is nowhere and everywhere? You're not making any sense. If I knew all of this then I wouldn't be asking you."

Well do the work. Think about it. Think about a place in your world, your reality, where there can be empty space. A place parallel to your world that can hold everything and nothing.

Jane thinks on Alice's words, rubbing her head and trying to stimulate an answer for these mind-bending questions she hears.

She thinks "There isn't a place where nothing and everything can exist, Alice. I really wish you start making some sense so I could understand how the hell to get out of here."

That's wrong. There is a place. Once you figure out what or where that place is, then you will figure out where you are and how to leave. You are in that space. That space in between everything and nothing.

Q. IMAGINE

Jane shouts "Alice.... I don't know. I need you to tell me!"

You'll figure it out. You have some time. Use it.

She tries to console herself from her building rage. Trying to focus on where she is and what Alice is trying to tell her, but her emotions get the best of her as she gives up and opens her mouth to wail her emotions out.

She throws her arms above her head and tries to scream to the top of her lungs, attempting to wail out every built-up emotion she has ever had in her body. When the moment of release comes, she sees a stream of red flow into the bottom of her pelvis. She's stunned to see a color not white in vast space but amazed as to how that is flowing from her.

Ahhh, you see now.

Jane says, "I see but I don't understand."

You will.

"How can I see my scream but not hear it?"

Maybe where you are, you don't need to produce things from your mouth.

"So, in this world." Jane pauses as she contemplates her next thought. "I only need my mind."

You always need your mind. And soul.

"Whatever. So, if I only need my mind for this world then my mind is how I can get out of this world?"

That is up to you.

"Alice, give me an answer." Jane begs.

Think. You have the answers.

"I'm thinking Alice but nothing is clicking! What are you saying? What is this?!"

I'm saying that you need to think. Since it is all you can do in this world. Use it. What this is will come to you once you think. If not think, feel. Feel what you are feeling right now.

Jane starts to concentrate on her current emotions and feelings.

"I feel angry!" Jane says. "I'm angry that you're not helping me. I'm angry that I don't understand everything you say. It's just making me more confused and I feel lost. I'm afraid. I'm feeling a whole list of emotions I can't even describe right now because they are hitting me all at once!"

The red stream starts to come back flowing from her pelvis, allowing Jane to start to put the pieces together.

She asks, "Is that my emotion?"

Yes.

"So, you can see emotion in this world?"

Yea Jane. In this world and your world.

Jane laughs and says, "But in this world. It flows in colors."

In both worlds it flows in colors. You just see it clearly here.

"Because everything else is white like a canvas. A blank page just waiting to be written on."

Jane thinks for a moment trying as she processes all of these things she's hearing and learning.

She then asks, "Is this my mind?"

See what time does Jane. You thought you would never figure out the answer and you did.

"I'm in my head" she says to clarify.

Correct.

"Why is it white?"

Because this is your realm of creation. Your blank canvas. Anything that would exist, exists here but only if you think about and when you think about it.

"So where are my memories?"

Here

"Where?"

Here and there. Everywhere and nowhere.

"How can I see them?"

Think of them.

Jane begins to think about one of her past birthdays where her theme was a celebrity showdown. She remembers the costumes all of her friends wore along with the games they played. The thrill of letting her imagination become engulfed in another persona yet hold true to her spirit when competing in games.

As Jane imagines the images of one of her birthday parties, it appears out of vast blank space as she opens her eyes. She sees her younger self and all of her friends on that beautiful spring day at the park. The rows of tables covers in confetti style table covers and layered with plates and juice boxes. The sounds of the barbecue sizzling in the background as she runs around playing kickball with her friends. She smells the shish kabob and hamburgers on the grill as she's running around the bases. As she hears her parents conversing with the other parents as she makes her way for a home run. She watches her team cheer for her when she makes it back. The corral of kids cheering and praising as they set up for the next person.

"What the...." she thinks.

You see now.

Jane is baffled by the sight of her memories as she stumbles to describe what she sees. "How is that...? It just... that's incredible."

I'm glad you like it.

"So, thoughts just appear when thought of in your mind?"

Yes. How else would they? When you think about them, don't you just think about them? They just appear, whenever and wherever they do. It's wondrous. This is how things become what they become. Through thoughts and energy.

"Energy?"

Yea Jane. The world you live in was at one point nothing.

Through spontaneous energy, it was created and made into something. Earth. The world you live in now wouldn't be the way it was if energy didn't shape the planet and humans didn't shape society through thoughts. It's all about energy and what you put towards something.

Jane begins to press against her head to stop the sudden throbbing.

"So, what you're telling me is that humans thought up the world. That's what you're saying?"

No. Humans thought up society.

"Okay Alice. How is this relevant to me and my situation right now?"

That you will have to figure it out.

Jane's patience runs out and she loses it. "Are you kidding me Alice? How can you spew these innuendos and say figure it out? Tell me!"

Jane waits for Alice's response.

"Hello? "She asks.

She realizes that she's completely left to her solitude with little knowledge gained and more questions that she could ask. Frustrated and feeling lost, she begins to think of a time she spent with her family during one of the Christmas holiday.

She was about eight years old and Marcus was five. It was the morning of Christmas and Marcus ran into Jane's room to try and wake her up to open gifts. She remembers being awake before Marcus barged in and begins to watch it in the blank space. The anticipating thrill of opening gifts and seeing what Santa gave her kept her wide awake and impatiently waiting for morning.

She watches as if she's watching a home video of her life. As her brother runs into her room and halts on his breaks when he sees she's already up. She stands in front of him in her satin pink night gown while Marcus is in his checkerboard pajamas. As she says to him, "Let's go wake them up?" as they sprint out of Jane's room and run down the stairs. They pass the tree stacked with gifts and sprint into a dive onto their parents' bed.

She smiles gleefully as she watches the joy of jumping onto her parent's bed, scaring the daylights out of their parents and enjoying every minute of it. She remembers her father picking her up and tickling her as sweet revenge while her mother gets at Marcus.

As tears start to fall from her eyes as she sees her entire family, sitting in the dining room next to the Christmas tree. Her mom finishing breakfast and making the household favorites like scrambled eggs, pancakes and crispy maple bacon. She heads into the dining room with the plates of food as she watches her children tear apart the wrapping around their boxes of gifts.

"That was the year I got the kitchen set." she says.

Her purple kitchen set was complete with plates, cups and silverware that she adored. She remembers the ecstatic feeling she felt when she saw what she had been dreaming of having. As she smiles from ear to ear, overjoyed to the point of dancing and jumping around. Jane remembers hearing her Dad laugh and smile at their happiness. The joy of both of his kids loving their gifts as Billie watches with the same face filled with glee.

"Such a good Christmas", she says.

Q. IMAGINE

"I really need to get home."

"I need to get out before it's too late."

CHAPTER III

In a space where time is unrecognized, Jane is succumbed to the feeling of past moments. She has no inkling of how long it's been since Alice's disappearance or how long she has been in this place.

All she knows is what she can do.

Experience.

Relive.

The past memories of her life flood into the blank space. As she reminisces and thinks of all her favorite moments and watches them within this canvas. She's reliving her seventeen years of life and the emotions felt through certain parts of her young life.

She laughs at the fun moments she'd share with her friends. All of the high times felt at Uncle Sook's. All of the joy shared in those blissful moments. She weeps at the touching childhood moments she shared with her parents, feeling the tear of her heart as she watches smiles appear on their face. She admires all of the bonding moments with Marcus and how even the fights brought them closer together. She ultimately feels pride in the moments where she overcame her mistakes. The times in her life where adversity came and she walked past it.

Q. IMAGINE

All of these moments she had forgotten in the real world. Now we're the only thing she had to hold onto. Jane starts to see and realize the things she should have done different with her family. As regrets starts to flood into the memories which highlights all of the moments, she made mistakes.

"Damn. I need to make it out of this", she says. "There's so much more to do. So many things I haven't done yet. How am I supposed to know my dreams? My purpose? If I haven't had the chance to find it."

She thinks about her life and starts to watch the memories pass by, "I'm only seventeen. I haven't even lived a quarter of my life yet. I still have things I want to accomplish and things that I want to explore and write about."

Thoughts of the poem she read in Mr. Dimonte's class start to arise. She starts to see herself reading aloud 'Sally and the Stone'. As she recites some of the verses, it pops out in her head.

"And Sally was all alone. She had nothing but the stone"

She thinks. "Maybe this is my stone."

Jane starts to dream about her poem instead of remembering it. She closes her eyes and thinks about all of the possibilities of who Sally could become and ultimately who she wanted to be.

Her thoughts running wild in her mind start to excite her and take her away from the grim reality of her canvas.

She starts to imagine how Sally would look and what drove her to be so cold and hateful in her life.

Jane's thought of Sally and the dimensions of her character start to take a hold of her mind. As she ponders the relevance of the stone and the significance of him leaving.

Then suddenly.

Out of her throat.

A bright blue beam shoots out and widens into the white space. Through the bright beam stems a figure of a woman.

As the bean begins to fade, her shape becomes more defined. Her black dress is more prominent and her long brown hair starts to shape her face. Her eyes gleam through the fading light as she stands in front of Jane and holds an ocean blue stone.

Jane steps back in awe, dumbfounded by the appearance of this woman.

As Sally is just as shocked as Jane is. She looks at herself in amazement and takes in the form she holds.

"This is interesting." Sally says.

She holds the stone up to her dark eyes to gaze into it and take in its beauty. As she holds the stone in the palm of her hand and is astounded by all of the characteristics it holds within its smooth sides.

The captivation of the stone wears off as she lifts her head and notices Jane.

Intrigued, Sally makes the gesture back and begins to laugh when she quickly snaps out of her astonishment.

"I second that interesting comment." Jane says.

Sally says "Indeed. I was once words on a page and now…. I'm this."

She glances at her skin and starts to touch her hair. To get to know this figure and this form.

As she says, "I was never this. I never really saw my stone before. I just knew I loved it and that it was always with me."

She looks at her stone and says, "But now I see it and now I know it's true beauty. It's amazing!"

She frolics at the joy of seeing her stone, swaying through the blank and leaving a sparkly trail with every step she takes.

Jane is amazed by the movement and joy of her character. So joyful, she begins to frolic through the blank space as well.

Jane leaves a solid green trail with her movements as she frolics and smiles gleefully and says to Sally, "I have a gift for you."

Jane closes her eyes as the blue beam begins to appear from her stomach. The beam shines next to Sally in the form of a man. It reveals as it fades, the tall and handsome man that captivates Sally away from her stone. As the beam fades away, the handsome man in all green stares directly at his skin and his form. Like Sally did.

"I was words" he says as he feels his skin and his clothes.

He turns his attention towards Sally, surprised to see another form like himself within this white space. Though his confusion fades into familiarity as his eyes gaze over to Sally when he notices the stone in her hand.

He looks into her eyes as she looks deep into his. And they move closer together as if drawn towards each other. They stand close enough to wear their bodies touch.

A stroke of the cheek sparks the first contact these long-lost lovers have ever had. The caressing of each other's face and skin starts to familiarize each other with who they are to each other.

The man in green says as he gazes into her eyes, "I know you. I think I do."

Sally gazes back at Jane and then turns towards him as she says, "I know you too. You left me with this beautiful stone."

"I wasn't happy about that especially the part that you left."

He says, "I don't know why I left or where I went. All I know is that I wasn't happy and neither were you."

Jane replies to the both of them, "You left her so she can find happiness within herself and grow whole. He had to leave for you to do that Sally."

They look at Jane and then look at each other as they try and process what they're hearing and what this all means. Sally starts to feel the handsome man caress her on her cheek which makes her pulls away and focus on her stone.

She says, "I have my stone and I have myself so I don't need you anymore."

Sally walks away into the white space, capturing one more glance of the handsome man before looking at her stone and drifting into the distance.

Q. IMAGINE

Her body fades into the white space which sets him into a panic.

"Where is my happiness now?" he says.

Jane thinks and closes her eyes again, imagining a way to make him happy as well. The blue beam appears again and shines to one of his hand. A stone appears on his hand when the bean fades away. Its thick black strides running through the smooth green texture grasp his attention for a moment. Until Jane thinks of Sally and she appears into the white space.

For the man in green to look at her as Jane says "Look! He has a stone now too."

Sally looks at his stone and notices its beautiful color and smooth texture. She blatantly says, "Good. Now he has something to make him whole."

He says as he puts his stone away, "I don't think this stone makes me whole."

 "I think I am whole even without the stone. Because I feel the same as I did before it even appeared."

Sally says in defense, "Well I need the stone to feel whole. I need it since you left. I'm afraid of it not being within my hands."

Jane smiles as she starts to shed clarity to the situation, figuring out what needs to be done and said.

She says, "Sally. The stone doesn't make you whole. You make you whole. The stone is a representation of what you thought your soul was before and how you thought you couldn't love anyone because you were cold. You needed the time to be by yourself to realize that you need people."

Jane continues, "Don't be mad at him. It had to happen that way or you both would have been miserable. Your independence gave you leeway to finding your heart. It gave you a path to finding out you can love since you loved that stone."

Sally begins to turn away from her stone and notice Jane and the handsome man next to her.

Jane says, "You are whole now even without the stone. You have enough love to give because now.... you love yourself. I created his stone and this man in order for you to not feel obliged to only be with your stone. To show your reflection since he now mirrors you."

Hearing Jane's words, Sally begins to smile as if now she has truly understood what happiness and love is. The man inches closer to Sally and reaches to caress her face. She looks towards him and places his hand on her face, gently gliding his fingers across her chin towards her lips. They stare into each other's eyes and relish on each other's faces, displaying all of the love they equally share and feel with or without the stones.

Jane looks at them in admiration for what she has done. Sally and the man begin to look at Jane and mirror the affection she displays towards them.

To her.

They turn away from Jane. in one small glance as she starts to walk into the blank space and fade from sight.

Instead of feeling saddened about being by herself again, Jane is overwhelmed with joy. She realizes within this blank world, she can see through her mind and into her mind.

Her memories.

Q. IMAGINE

Her fantasy.

Her work.

All of her dreams and aspirations that she wants to create. Jane starts to relish on what Alice has been saying to her.

"Maybe this is everything and nothing."

Alice appears.

So now you know...

Jane smiles and agrees, "Yes Alice. Now I know."

So now that you know, what are you going to do about it?

Jane giggles and begins to frolic through the blank. She says in a state of bliss, "I don't know yet and I don't mind not knowing. I have time to figure it out"

Yes Jane, for now.

CHAPTER IV

Jane's mind start to go on a parade of imagination and wonder as she creates visions of worlds and places. She lives within these paradoxes as she wanders through her mind. Her imagination expands to the depths of space as it shifts from mystical worlds and magical creatures to the modern landscapes in the real world.

She imagines herself in the vast Sahara Desert treading through the mountainous sand dunes and trying to balance her weight on the camel she rides. Her body moves with the pace of the animal, feeling its slow strides and rocking movements in each step. The blue berber nomad turban she wears protects her face from the heat of the sun along with the brutal force of the sand.

Jane sees nothing but the blue sky and the mountainous dunes in this ever-expanding desert. She thinks of creating an oasis and some mystical land of life. As if it's hidden within this barren ground that could save her from boredom.

Yet her interests start to wander into a more tropical place. She starts to envision as she hops off the camel and walks down one of the dunes.

She slides down the dune and starts to reach water once her feet land at the bottom. The vision of the desert starts to diminish as she stumbles over a shallow creek embedded in roots and brush.

The envisionment of the tropical Amazon rainforest starts to take ahold of her mind. She projects the encapsulation of wimba trees over her head that allow small fragments of light and sky within their vast canopies. Jane pulls out a machete to chop down any vine that comes in her path, keeping her ears out for jaguars and watching her step for snakes.

The moisture in the air starts to weigh down her chest as she hikes through the ever-growing jungle. The intense heat encourages her to find a seat and rest on the one of the roots embedded in the ground. She pulls out a water filled canister to stay hydrated along with some fruit to snack on as she enjoys the view of such an abundant place. Noting how the enclosure of trees tends to shade the beautiful nature lingering within.

Jane loves the beauty of the massive wimba trees. She compares the glimpses of the sky seen through the canopy to rivers and streams seen on a geographical map. The hints of blue light flowing through the cracks of green and brown. As it makes its way through the spaces it can fit in.

She says as she gazes into the canopy "As above, so below."

The admiration of the scenery holds her attention for a little while. But like the Sahara Desert, she grows tiresome of the masterpiece and starts to brainstorm herself to another slice of her imagination.

She sifts through her memory of scenes she has seen and imagined in her lifetime, stopping at the images of prairies and large fields of grass. The images are similar to the vastness of the Sahara, except with life flowing through its soil and hills of green and tall grass.

She steps over the tree roots of the Amazon and into the tall grass covering most of the Great Plains. She looks beyond the line that cuts the sky from the land. She travels as far as her eyes can see in this place of enrichment.

And to her surprise as she walks through the tall grass pastures, she stumbles across a herd of buffalo grazing on the tall grasses and trampling to other hills.

Though the sun begins to set and create a hazy brown shadow over the grass. The shadow lengthens and become darker as the sun starts to obscure behind the hills. Jane lays on the fields of grass, breathing in the fresh open air and smells of the blooming flowers. She watches the color show in the sky as the setting sun turns the sky from its tranquil blue to calming shades of purple, pink and orange.

She closes her eyes and listens to the sound of the wind, hearing the wind blow through the grass and create a symphony among the plants living here. Jane loses herself to the calming sounds of the prairie. She floats her mind on the symphony until the sounds of the Great Plains suddenly fall silent. As her mind fully grasps the image of the Great Plains, yet she only hears silence once her eyes close.

When her eyes open, she is revealed to be in the blank white space. The familiarity of nothing put a distaste in her mouth as she reminisces on her adventures.

"And I almost forgot."

Disappointed on the fact that it was only a dream, she tries to remain positive and proud. Her mind expanded farther than she had ever thought it could, though the expansion was all internal.

Q. IMAGINE

"That one lasted longer than the others." She says.

Being able to vividly remember and live. Every inch of the world crossing her mind. Images she has seen in her real life whether on TV or in person. She tries to become grateful for the memories and images she holds, especially since it's the only thing that's helping her bare the reality of her situation.

Her memories and dreams are as accurate as the actual act of witnessing these wondrous landscapes and seeing and experiencing the vivid beauty they hold. There unique sceneries that make them so memorable and captivating.

Jane thinks, "I'm going to get out of here and see these places. Even the ones I have seen before. I just need to figure out how to get out of my head. This place is limiting my time."

Alice appears.

Who is limiting your time?

"Life. This place." Jane says.

How is life limiting your time?

Jane gets attuned to the innuendos of Alice and starts to really think about the meaning behind the words instead of how the words are said.

"Because I can't get out of here Alice. I have no idea how dreaming and remembering is going to get me out of this place. And life is short. How am I to know I'll be able to go to these places when I get out? If I get out? I don't know."

Indeed, time is limited in your reality. And this reality. But the future is full of possibilities. Some good and some bad. It's just a matter on what you focus on. What you believe will happen.

"Well how am I to know I'll have a chance? How am I to know if I'll be able to go back if I can't even figure out how to get out of my head."

Believe and think. Imagine yourself out of here and believe that it will happen. The only time that exists in this current moment is the now. The past has already happened and the future is to be written by your current actions. Use the time you have now to figure out what you desire. Keep going. You're getting closer.

"I don't know Alice. I'm tired of this. I want to leave but I have no idea how to leave. Leaving your mind is not something I've ever done before. Especially with the amount I smoked. This really was my stomping grounds.... but now I'm trapped."

If you believe you're trapped then you will be trapped. Keep traveling through your thoughts Jane. Your memories. And you will find what you seek.

Jane listens to Alice and starts to shuffle through her mind to certain moments in her life. Her mind travels to more moments spent with Marcus. The times where Marcus and she were at a sleep away camp and left their cabins one morning to catch the sunrise.

She closes her eyes and calms down her thoughts to the images of that dark morning they left their log cabins. She becomes engulfed in the memory and starts to watch her 13-year-old self find Marcus sneaking out to meet her. The morning dew on the grass starts to dampen their sneakers as they walked through the forest. They fill their lungs with the moist air of the morning. As they tip toe through the camp site in order to prevent their camp counselors from awakening. They try to be as quiet as their surroundings to evade being caught.

Their lanterns helped aid their way to the beach lake as they watch out for any wolves and bears. Excitement jolts through their heart as they make it safely past their camp site and closer to the beach lake. Their eyes gleaming with joy as the sound of the lake starts to become more present to their ears, passing the oak and pine trees they have been dodging for the past few minutes.

They turn their eyes to the sounds of the lake hitting the shore. The sight of waves floating towards them as the brisk wind blows in their face.

The sun begins to rise as they take their sneakers off and step up onto the dock for a better view. They sit next to each other and observe the changes in the sky as the sun begins to rise. Marcus leans his head on his sister's shoulder and Jane leans her head on his. Current Jane smiles from afar as she watches the touching moment that. She begins to miss that close relationship they once held and regrets how things have changed.

Jane begins to hold her chest and gasp from the pain she feels as a green stream starts to shine through.

"I need to see my family. I need to see Marcus." She says.

Alice appears.

It will happen before you know it. Just relax and honor your life.

"Honor my life for what?" Jane asks.

Honor your life because you may still live.

Jane fades away from this pleasant memory of her and her

brother watching the sunrise. She turns this beautiful scenic moment into a serene beach setting. As she watches the waves of the Pacific Ocean wash up ashore on the island of Maldives. The pain begins to fade as she feels the powdery white sand sliding in between her toes. The tropical sun beats onto her skin as she slips into a tranquil moment to enjoy tanning her honey brown skin into a deep mocha color.

She lounges out in a blue bikini and a sun hat, shading her face from the rays of the sun and sipping on a coconut cupped drink. Jane splurges on her fantasy as she imagines two handsome men fanning her glistening body. Each of them bronze and glistening in the sun as they rhythmically fan her.

She takes one last sip out of the fuzzy coconut before putting it down and laying on her back. She enjoys the sun rays on her back and the cool breeze from the fans. She relishes in the relaxation of the beach and the calming sounds of the ocean feeling serene in the moment. Although her mind keeps trying to float to images of Marcus and that time at the lake.

While Jane sits on her fantasized beach in her fantasy of the Maldives, her family within the real world is fracturing due to the distress of their daughter's or sister's state of health. The family dynamic has been collapsing like a row of dominoes after Jane was kidnapped and found in a comatose state.

Marcus sits in Jane's room directly in front of her bed. His back is pushed up against his backpack on the chair as she stares at Jane from across the room. His eyes are bloodshot and droopy from all the tears he has been shedding over the past couple of weeks. The fatigue from his sleepless nights are demonstrated on his face as broad darkened circles and wrinkles form under his eyes. Marcus looks as if he has aged 40 years in only 3 weeks and his lack of concern can be seen on his face.

His normal sly look that he keeps posted within his smile diminishes into a hateful and deadly stare. As he's begun to dread the world he has to walk through while resenting any glimpse of happiness that floats his way. He holds the little energy he has left into that pernicious stare towards her. He leans back into his chair with a look of disgust directed towards his sister. As if he's patiently waiting for her to wake up just so he can unleash all of his feelings pent up towards her in an instant.

While he patiently stares at his sister and waits for her emergence to occur, Jane is relaxing within her mind and enjoys the state of peace she has found in this space. Although images of Marcus still pop into her serene space, she finds comfort in the present moment of her imagination, focusing her energy on finding relaxation.

Marcus, at the hospital, stands up out of the chair and walks closer to Jane. He sits on the side of her bed and continues to stare at her with a look one gives to his mortal enemy. He says, "You need to wake up Jane. I'm tired of this."

As he removes his backpack and places it on the bed, he says, "You were my salvation in this world besides Neal."

He sniffles as he begins to mutter the words, "But you're my only chance in this world of inconsistencies. You're all I have now since love is dead, Jane."

He begins to unzip his backpack as tears drip onto his clothes. As he reaches into his backpack until his emotions overwhelm him and he sobs ferociously.

He yells, "I have no one else to make the pain go away Jane! No one to make this world a little brighter. No one. Nothing. All because I ran away, I just…couldn't be that man."

He begins to pound on his skull in order to force the tears away. "Stop crying! I'm so sick of crying. Stop crying. I'm tired. Stop being weak."

A nurse enters the room after hearing Marcus rant from the hallway.

"Is everything okay?" she asks.

Marcus quickly wipes away his tears and turns his face towards the nurse.

"Yes, ma'am. Everything is fine. I'm just talking to my sister."

He tries to brighten up his voice in order to ensure the nurse that everything is okay. She turns away and closes the door.

The nurse leaves the room thinking everything is normal and the boy was just grieving. And in her mind, what she just witnessed was a young boy grieve for his sister. Though when she leaves the room, she has no idea of the unfortunate truth. That Marcus is not grieving and she is wrong.

CHAPTER V

Within her fantasy, Jane rotates on her back to try and even out the tan. She enjoys listening to the sounds of the waves briskly hitting the shoreline as the breeze from the water caresses her face. She feels the sun beat on her back as the fanboys continue with their rhythmic fanning.

You can see the serenity she feels on her face as she maintains her mind within this dream. She focuses on the peaceful space she has imagined herself in along with all of its luxuries.

Yet to her surprise, it was not her mind that aided in her drift from this peaceful moment. Those moments of tranquility she was convinced to feel after seeing a heartfelt memory.

As the beach remains present in her mind, and the fanboys continue to fan her glistening body, the calming feeling starts to fade as she sees something wading in the distant shoreline. Jane notices the image out of the corner of her eye. She hones in on the image as it becomes more present in the distance. She lifts up her glasses to try and make out the shadowy image from afar, determining if the shadow is a mirage from the heat or actually present.

Meanwhile at the hospital, Marcus tries to control his emotions to prevent any more outbursts and any unwarranted attention. He starts to pep talk himself out of his motives for visiting Jane.

"This is crazy. I don't even know what I'm doing right now."

He lays his head on Jane as he begins to sob from the pain. "I don't know what else to do anymore. I just…. can't feel this anymore. It's too much."

Marcus looks up at his sister's resting face. The peaceful expression hidden behind her sleeping eyes. The subtle movements of her chest that lets him know she is still here. While her mind wanders through the dimensions of her realm of creation.

"I need you to wake up sis." he says as he begins to caress her face. "I know you are still here but I need you here with me. In this world."

He watches Jane as she lays in her bed only to see the subtle lifting of her chest and the beeping from the monitor to let him know she's still here. He then reaches for his backpack and begins to unzip. His breath starts to get heavy as the opening widens and reveals what he has in store.

He looks towards the door and window to make sure he's not being watched. For what he wants to do. What he is going to do. He needs no witnesses.

Jane patiently watches the figure without taking her eyes off of it. She waits to see any movement, any inkling that the image is coming closer. She wonders what it is and why it lingers within the distance but instead of focusing on the shadow, she maintains her fantasy and tries to find that serenity she once felt.

Q. IMAGINE

After unzipping his backpack, Marcus quickly gets up and locks the door.

Ensuring their privacy.

No disturbances.

He walks back to the bed and pulls out a small black kit and a spoon from his backpack. He opens the kit up and pulls out a glass vile filled with a white substance, a syringe, a tourniquet and a torch lighter.

"Can't hide for long Jane" he says. "Time to wake up."

Jane blames the shadowy figure on dehydration from the sun and puts the image out of her mind.

"It's probably just my imagination running."

After torching the powdery substance on the spoon, Marcus fills his syringe with the serum and starts to check for air bubbles.

He pauses before putting the needle to his arm to glance at her one last time.

"Why couldn't you just have woken up huh? Why can't you just be there for me? You don't know what it was like to be at Neal's funeral."

He puts the needle to his arm and says, "Maybe I'll see you on the other side. Maybe I'll meet you before me and Neal are together again."

He starts to insert the needle into his vein and inject the serum.

"It'll be me and you in the fantasy world. One last time like the good ol days."

As he pulls out the needle, he instantly begins to roll his eyes to the back of his head. His body falls next to the side of his sister and he starts to snuggle her in his arms.

"Me and you. Just us two."

Jane wakes out of her tranquil state when she feels an eerie feeling in the pit of her stomach. She turns on her back to get up out of the lounge chair when she sees the shadowy figure heading towards her.

Jane quickly removes her sunglasses to get a better picture when she sees the shadow define itself into a masculine figure and head directly for her. The man walks aggressively at her which prompts Jane to signal her fan boys to stop him.

She watches them walk up to the distant man and sees before her eyes. Her fan boys dissipate within the air after contact. Jane's mind begins to fill with fear as the man continuously walk towards her and increases her pace.

"Who are you?" she yells.

As he approaches, his face becomes obscured by the hat he wears. He doesn't respond when Jane asks to identify himself, prompting Jane to take this encounter as an unfriendly one.

She closes her eyes and imagines the man disappearing from sight and being swept by the wave. And as soon as she envisions it within her mind, a tidal wave forms off the shoreline and plunges on top of the man, obscuring her view of him and his view of her.

The wave flows back into the ocean and reveals Jane's plan did not work. The stranger is now a few feet away as Jane tries to make out the face hidden under the hat.

Within arm's reach, he reaches out to grab her forcefully. He clenches handfuls of air as she swiftly moves away from his grasp. He lands a hand on her arm and tries to pull her closer to him until Jane imagines herself as a martial artist and begins to fight herself free of his grasp.

She starts to throw roundhouse kicks with her feet, blocking his wings with her arms. They fight until she finally lands one fierce kick on his chest. Once she knocks him off of his feet and he falls into the sand, she sees this as an opportunity to get away and sprints down the shoreline. She turns her martial art skills into the ancient skills of a Japanese warrior as she imagines herself hiding on one of the rooftops housing a zen garden in the middle. As the dim night sky aids Jane's allure, she patiently waits and searches for any movement within the garden. While she waits to see if he'll reveal himself, she whispers to herself "What is going on?"

Jane looks into the dim sky and says "Alice if you're around. Is this a test or something?"

She quickly focuses her attention on the garden as she hears a scuffle near the bushes. The stranger jumps out from behind a bush hidden in the opaque night and leaps towards Jane on the roof. As he glides towards her, she pulls out a ninja star and flings it at him, hearing the impact of the star impaling him and forcing him to fall towards the ground.

She looks to see if she can identify who he is. But his hat still obscures his face from his sight. She decides her only means of salvation is to keep running. So, she jumps off of the roof and begins to fly away into another fantasy and another form.

Back at the hospital, Marcus talks to Jane in his delirious state of mind.

"The worst part about all of this is that I never got to tell you how much I love you. How much I need you and miss hanging out with you. But I guess that's a family trend, you know. To live in regret for how you treat the people you love."

He curls closer towards her and starts to rest his head next to hers.

"Now I know why you numb yourself so much. It is better to live in the clouds."

Jane spreads her arms out and imagines them sprout feathers. She soars through the sky as her body starts to transform into a majestic golden eagle. She glides over the Cascade Mountain range with the magnetism and appeal every eagle portrays in flight.

Her eyesight is sharp as she hones in on the smallest of creatures walking the earth. They dash from every angle and search anything that moves or anything that resembles that man.

While looking for the stranger, she spots a squirrel and swoops down to clasp it with her talons. The creature squirms within her tight grip as she squeezes the squirrel tighter before taking flight. As she searches for a spot to harvest her catch, she finds a nest to release the squirrel.

And as she feels an animal instinct to fiercely jab at it with her beak, she hears a strange noise which catches her senses. What sends her into a frantic state of shock is the sound of a nearby gunshot. She quickly lifts up out of her nest as it disappears before her eyes into scattered pieces. The hay and twigs fly into her face as she looks down to see the stranger holding the rifle in the air towards her. Jane dives behind a mountain and skims above the ground, only to turn her flight into a high-speed sprint.

Her sharp talons turn into long, impregnable legs. Their beautifully encapsulated in golden fur black spots and moving faster than she has ever moved in her life. She begins to feel her tufts of fur flow through the air as she runs through the Masai Mara as a cheetah. She's never felt her body move at such a velocity as her paws barely touch the hot ground. She runs through the tall patches of grass and looks for a place to hide as she hears the engine of a truck in the distance. She sprints towards another patch of tall grass before hearing the voracity of gunshots sounding off from behind. The truck starts to speed up and get closer towards her, making her switch fantasies again.

Desperate for her life, she sprints away and squinches her eyes close. She imagines herself far away from this stranger as she leaps into the air and falls into a body of water. She can feel her body sink down to the depths of the ocean as her legs beginning to flail like a fish tail as she swims further away from the light of the surface.

She glides through the water over the bedrock sand, looking around in the dark murky water to ensure she's not being followed. Jane notices a large dark mass at the bottom of the sea and swims closer to get a better look. The dark mass starts to reveal itself in the form as a sunken ship that's slowly decaying from the weight of the ocean and sea life around it.

As Jane swims closer to the shipwreck, Marcus starts to float in and out of consciousness. He says to her, "Jane. I hope I see you when you pass on but I know I'll see you before I see Neal."

He runs his fingers through her matted locks of hair and starts to smile. In one final moment, he says "I'll see you before I'm free."

His eyes close as he lets the weight of his body drag him off of the bed and onto the floor. His fingers caught in her hair forces Jane's head to jerk with his body and hand off of the bed. The sudden movement forces the leads on her chest and the IV to eject out, spewing blood all over her and causing the monitor to sound off.

As Jane swims to the shipwreck, she feels a sudden tug of her hair from behind her. As the tug jerks her entire body backwards, the familiar sensation flashes her mind back to the blank space. She stands and watches an unfamiliar memory that shows an image of herself and a forgotten man, shackled and tortured in a forgotten space.

The images of the creepy man fondling her under her dress sinks a dreadful feeling in her chest. She turns away. Jane is astonished at what her mind reveals to her eyes, resurfacing an array of thoughts and feelings she never knew existed.

The nurse tries opens the door to check on the machine but the lock on the inside prevents her from gaining access.

She says to one of the nurses behind the desk, "I need a master key. The door is locked and the patient's machine is sounding off."

The nurse behind the desk stands up and walks over with the master key for all of the hospital doors. She unlocks the door and starts to walk away, until the other nurse gasps in fear at the sight of Jane's head and torso lopsided off of the bed.

"We have a situation here." she yells.

The two nurses sees her hair deeply threaded in between Marcus' fingers as his body lies limp on the side of her bed. Drool drips out of his mouth as blood spurts out of Jane's arm. His eyes lay tightly shut while Jane's face is obscured by her hair.

The two nurses acquire the attention of the other nurses on the floor. As they convene in front of the door momentarily before quickly accessing the stability of the patient and the boy.

One of the nurse's lifts Marcus up and untangles his hand out of her hair. She places two fingers on his throat before yelling to the remaining nurses "Someone notify the doctor! We need a crash cart and a gurney. Right now!"

One of the nurses sprints out of the room and searches the hallway for a doctor. While the nurse who barged in on Marcus before, lifts up Jane and tries to stop the bleeding from her arm. She manually takes her pulse and respiration before yelling, "We need another crash cart."

The nurse on the floor with Marcus spots the black kit under the bed. She sees a scattered amount of glass on the floor with an empty used syringe holding center within the sharp fragments.

"Holy shit. We really have a problem here."

A doctor barges through the door and stands appalled by the massacre of blood soaking the sheets and the visitor lying unconscious on the floor.

"What the hell is going on here!", he yells.

"Sir, we opened the door and saw the patient hanging off of the bed with this boy pulling her down by her hair. He may have yanked the leads off of her and sounded the monitor off. He also yanked the IV out of her causing this massacre of blood."

"And what the hell happened to him?", he asks.

"We don't know sir. It looks like a possible drug overdose." says the nurse holding up Marcus. "I called Nurse Ida to get me the crash cart. His pulse is showing abnormalities."

The doctor looks at the nurse helping Jane and says, "Karen, hook her back up to the monitor." He then looks back at the one on the floor and says, "Chantelle, check his pupils. We might have to page another doctor or send him to the ER."

As Chantelle lift his eyelids up to see his pupils, the doctor leans over to Chantelle to get a look for himself. The pupils were the severely dilated to the size of a pencil point.

Doctor yells outside of the room, "Where's that crash cart and gurney?"

"Chantelle, how's his breathing?"

"Shallow sir. I barely feel his chest lifting up." she says.

"Ida, where are you!?" he yells back into the hallway.

"Sorry doctor, I had to go to the next floor to get the gurney." she says hustling through the door.

She jumps right in to help Chantelle lift Marcus on the gurney.

Q. IMAGINE

The doctor demands, "Bring him to the drug and alcohol unit and get a Naloxone injection ready and a banana bag. While their still some time and get one of the other nurses to notify his family. Do we know who he is?"

Nurse Karen just finishes the re insertion of the IV and begins to stick new leads on her chest. She says, "It's her brother, Sir."

She hooks Jane up to the monitor to hears the machine blare out sirens about her vitals. The doctor and the nurse look at the monitor as it shows her heart rhythm resembling the image of a child scribbling.

He yells, "She's in V-fib! Where's that crash cart Ida?!"

Ida runs back into the hallway while the doctor starts to manually perform CPR.

He says to her while fiercely pushing on her chest "C'mon Jane. Don't quit now."

Jane stares into the blank space baffled by the images she just saw. She has no recollection of being in an abandoned storage container and being bound by her wrist. She doesn't remember breaking her wrist to get free or kicking various men in the genitals. She has no idea how she skillfully dodged henchman to reach salvation or managed to be alive after feeling the icy chill of the river.

"How could I forget something like that?" she says putting her head down as she curls into a ball. She remains in that position, trying to forget the memories she just re lived until she hears her name.

"Jane?"

Jane slowly lifts up her head to the familiar voice and faces the approaching shadow walking in her direction.

"I'm not running anymore", she says as she stands to her feet.

She patiently watches the figure reveal himself before her eyes. As she asks, "Who are you?"

The figure reveals his tall and lanky teenage built with a large curly fro and a reminiscent smile.

He says, "How could you forget me after 3 weeks sis?"

Marcus stands before her dressed completely in white, looking impeccable as he smiles gleefully towards her. Jane stares at him and hesitantly reaches out to touch him. Fearing he is a part of her imagination and will disappear, she lays one finger on him. She feels his smooth texture and warm skin. Until he jumps and starts to shriek in fear, falling towards the ground and closing his eyes upon impact.

"Marcus!" Jane yells. "Oh No! No no no." she says.

Marcus turns his fearful behavior into a jokingly one, laughing hysterically as he opens his eyes and sees the expression on Jane's face.

"You fool!" he says. "Had to do something to get you back."

Jane jumps on him and hugs him dearly. Gripping him so tightly, her arms start to hurt.

"You don't know how long I've been waiting to do that." she says.

"I do. I really do." he says, struggling to speak from Jane's tight grip.

Jane loosens up her grip to look at her brother, stunned by his appearance in this realm she thought was only hers.

"How are you here Marcus?" she says rubbing his fro. "How did you even get here?"

Marcus looks around and says "I don't know. I was following this woman and she led me here."

Jane looks surprised. "What woman?" she asks.

"I don't know. It's hard to explain."

Nurse Karen brings Marcus into one of the rooms in the drug and alcohol unit, signaling to the technicians that this patient needs a Naloxone injection and an ECG monitoring his heart.

She says, "He also needs an IV drip but set up the injection first."

She stands back and watches the technicians do their work in hopes they can work quick enough to save him.

Back in Jane's room, Ida comes back with the crash cart.

"Got the crash cart" says Ida.

"It's about damn time." the doctor replies. He switches from manual compressions to hook up the crash cart.

"One of you open the gown and gel the pads", he says as he warms up the defibrillator.

Ida cuts open the gown with scissors as Karen gels the pads and places them on her chest.

"Pads gelled and in place." she says.

Marcus explains to Jane, "I don't know what happened really. All I remember is I went to see you and then I saw this bright light take over me. I was spinning in it like I was flying. Until I saw this woman in a black dress. She came to me and gave me a stone then told me to give it to you."

Marcus opened up his hand and revealed a solid black stone with ocean blue waves gliding over the surface of it. Jane lifted up the stone and was mesmerized by the beauty of it. Although she recognized it as the same stone Sally had when she appeared into the blank space.

At the hospital, Chantelle and the technicians are working the IV and EKG monitoring Marcus' vitals. Chantelle gives him the injection as the technicians hook him up to the ECG and pulse ox.

One of them says, "Nurse, he's bradypneic and hypotensive."

"Hook him up to oxygen STAT!" she says.

Soon after the technician pulls put the oxygen mask and places it on his face, the EKG monitor blares.

"He's going into V-fib! Get the defibrillator ready!"

Jane is still mesmerized by the stone but she listens to Marcus as he explains the rest of the story.

"Then the weirdest occurrences happened and.... it's if I was living in a videogame or something. She ran away before I could ask her where you are or where I could find you."

She begins to listen intentively.

"Defibrillator is ready ma'am." says one of the technicians.

"Everyone stand clear!", the nurse says before she presses the button to start the electrical current.

Marcus says, "She was running....and I followed her. But it led me to a beach and instead of running she was just sitting there." Marcus explains.

Jane's looks of interest now turns into an expression of confusion.

After shocking Marcus with the defibrillator, his heart rhythm doesn't change.

"Patient is still in V-fib", the technician says.

"Ugh! Get me the paddles and someone page a doctor!" Chantelle says.

"Jane it was amazing!", he explains. "I was walking towards her until she sent these random guys towards me. They were holding me from walking any closer. So, I pushed them off and they evaporated! Into this iridescent dust! It was the coolest thing I've ever seen."

The doctor shocks Jane with the defibrillator only to see her heart rhythm had no changes and was still in Vfib.

"Get me the panels." he says to Karen.

Ida barges into the room. "Doctor, you're needed downstairs."

"Can't you see I'm busy right now. Go get another doctor." he yells.

The doctor starts to warm up the panels before telling Karen to turn up the voltage.

"It's this patient's brother. He's still in V-fib!", Ida shouts trying to get the doctor's attention.

"Clear!" he says before he shocks her body again.

"Still no changes, doctor!" Karen says.

"One more time!" He shouts

He notices Ida still standing there and says, "Ida, Go get another doctor! I can't be two places at once!"

Back in the blank space, Jane tries to put all of the puzzle pieces together.

"That was you Marcus?" Jane asks.

Q. IMAGINE

"That was me where Jane?" he asks. "I saw that women in the black dress, not you. I started to run towards her and she tries to kick my ass. Extremely confusing by the way."

"Clear", Chantelle says as Marcus' body jumps up out of the bed.

A steady flat sounds off in the room. Horrifying every nurse and technician present.

"He's flat-lining!" yells one of them.

"Oh...shit, shit. Shit! Where's the doctor? "Chantelle yells. "Charge me again!"

As Marcus continues his story "And I was blocking all of her moves. All of her kicks. She got me once though."

Jane can't help but rub her head since that story sounds like hers. Except that man wasn't Marcus.

The doctor in Jane's room starts to charge the panels one more time. "Charge is ready." Karen says, hoping for the best.

"CLEAR!", he yells. The charges surges through her body as she jerks up in the bed.

While Chantelle in the drug and alcohol unit hears one of the technicians say, "Charge is ready!"

She holds the panels to his chest and yells "CLEAR!"

Jane starts to focus on the story Marcus is telling her and her own fantasy. She turns away from him for a moment. Trying to process what's going on.

"How can this be so?" she asks. She tunes out Marcus' voice to think until she turns back around to ask, "Marcus. how.........."

As Jane turns around to see her brother, she winds up looking to the depths of white space. Marcus is nowhere to be found.

She calls out his name loudly but her voice is only met with silence.

She looks around and starts to run in circles. Running through the blank as she calls out his name. She stops and imagines herself back at the beach in the Maldives in hopes he will be there.

But when she focus on that scene, he isn't there. She travels to the other scenes. Through her other fantasies that he described in his story.

Nothing.

Jane yells, "Marcus? Marcus?" Pleading for an answer. She winds up back into the blank space, yelling his name and hoping to see an answer. Yet Marcus and his voice is nowhere to be found.

Jane is all alone and her brother is gone.

The doctor and Karen patiently waits to see her stabilize. To their relief, they did.

"She's back." he says as he wipes the sweat from his brow.

Downstairs with Nurse Chantelle and the technicians, a doctor walks in and says, "What's going on in here?"

Chantelle pressed the paddles on his chest and watches his body jump off of the gurney. The jerk makes her hopeful of a pulse. Yet she sees no change in rhythm. Just a flatline.

The doctor checks the vitals on the screen and his vitals manually. While everyone waits patiently for a glimmer of hope that this boy is still alive. Though hope is diminished when the doctor says, "Time of death 5:15."

"Marcus! Marcus! Marcus!" Jane shouts. She feels her body tire out from all the running so she sits down and begins to curl into a ball again. Her emotions intensify as she feels so confused about this whole ordeal her life has been.

I'm sorry Jane.

"What?" she yells.

It's time to let go. Time to wake up.

"What?" she asks again, speaking in a softer tone. Jane starts to feel a head rush as she loses balance and starts to fall through the blank space. She drifts through an array of colors and starts to feel the pressure of her chest and the brush of her breath. She hears people hovering over her from above, trying to make out the voices as her eyes begin to open. She sees a flash of light drifting from one to the other and the sound of a machine in the distance.

Beep

Beep

Beep

The beep starts to become more subtle as a man stands over and says, "Welcome back, Jane McKenzie."

CHAPTER VI

So, this is reality...

After a few days of rest and processing the things she has endured these past couple of days, Jane is ready and able to leave the confines of the hospital room that she has been in for the past few weeks. For the first time since she's been admitted, Jane can maneuver her body out of the bed and walk. She takes each step with precaution and uses the IV stand as a balance to stay afoot. She feels the lukewarm floor of her hospital room turn into the bitter icy cold tiles of her bathroom. As she quickly shuffles onto the bathmat and calms her feet down from the temperature change. She leans over to twist the knob for the shower but loses her balance and runs into the wall tile. Her body is so fragile and stiff that she needs to hold onto the IV pole every second or she'll end up hurting herself.

She gains her balance back and twists the knob to start the shower, turning the knob was supposed to be the most difficult part of washing up. Though she is re informed that the troublesome part would be removing her gown off of her body without ejecting the IV out of her arm.

"Who knew a simple task like taking a shower would be so difficult."

Before stepping into the shower, she decides to look at herself in the mirror, noting it has been awhile since she's seen her own image. Though what she sees when she looks in the mirror, is a pale version of herself that she barely even recognizes. The image of the girl dressed in her luau outfit was replaced with the image of a skinny and malnourished girl. She resembles a woman whom just made it back from the brinks. Her eyes and complexion showed the effects of a near demise. Her body and wounds show the brutal nature of what she had endured.

"I don't know this girl I see."

Jane steps into the warm sprinkling of water as her mind starts to feel an instant gratification for still being alive and having the ability of re live this sensation again. There was a freeing sensation being completely naked and unveiling the years and stories of her life. Though there was also a moment of being completely lost in the sensation of the shower.

She was just a girl. A person. Not a lucky individual or an abnormally strong person. Just a person. A creation. A mere spectacle in this vastness of the world and all that it held, as she just managed to stay alive.

She sits on the shower chair and immerses her body completely in the water, letting the warm sensation drip down her head and run to her toes. She breathes in the steam and feels her pores exfoliate.

After relishing in the warmth of the water for a while, she takes in how every moment of her life leads into this moment of peace right now. She begins to open up a bottle of shampoo and starts to wash herself clean of the image of the past.

"Out of this shower I will become anew."

Q. IMAGINE

She runs her fingers through her curls, untying the knots and seeing the revitalization of her hair.

"Now to work on the rest of me."

After spending an hour in the shower, relishing on the warm water and thinking about the things she wants to change. She has a second chance so she wants to make the best of it.

"Guess it's time to reveal thyself." she says as she turns the shower off and reaches for her towel. Her clean and refreshed skin starts to resemble the honey brown complexion she once held. Along with her hair resembling the curl pattern she once had. Those vivacious curves she once held that attracted everyone that glanced and looked, now resembles a small form of her old figure. Though she takes that image that is revealed to her in the mirror and says, "This is a beautiful starting point for me and I'm just glad to be alive."

She leans over to the basket sitting on top of the toilet seat as she feels her strength build up enough to avoid using the support of the IV pole. She grabs one of the lotions lying in the basket and starts to apply it on her skin. After a few minutes of moisturizing and lathering her body, she places her drabby gown on just in time for a knock on her door and the entering of her father.

He walks in gleefully after seeing the image of his daughter out of her bed and moving. The sight of her looking alive brings tears into his eyes accompanied with a gracious smile. He is truly grateful for her ability to keep moving forward through such a tumultuous time and shows his gratitude with every tear dripping down his face.

"Glad to see you up baby girl." he says trying to wipe his tears away. He places a bag of clothes on the chair in front of her bed and sojourns a glance on the chair, knowing that this was the last seat Marcus sat on before he passed on.

She quickly moves towards her dad and hugs him. The scent of his scented cologne and his strong built that she missed brings her to joy as she embraces him.

"I missed this." she says while squeezing him with all of her strength.

"I missed this too." he says back to her as he kisses her head and rubs her back in comfort.

"Did they say when I can get this thing out of my arm?" Jane asks.

He laughs enjoying her readiness to leave and says, "They said the IV technician will be here in a few moments to remove the IV."

To their surprise the IV technician knocks on the door in a moments time.

"Come in." Isaac says. Jane moves away from her father and sits back down for the IV tech to take this device out of her arm.

She sits patiently and watches the woman turn the IV machine off and skillfully remove the needle out of her arm. Jane doesn't even flinch at the prick she felt as the tip of the needle left her arm. As the IV tech puts pressure on the insertion site, another knock comes to the door.

Isaac opens the door to let in the food server stroll in shelves filled with trays of food. He says, "Glad to see you're up Ms. McKenzie. The doctor wanted you to get a meal in before you leave to see how you respond to solid foods."

Jane says quickly, "I think I'll respond to it just fine."

The server chuckles and places a large brown tray in front of her. Before he leaves, he lets Jane and her father know that the doctor will be in shortly to talk to her before she's discharged.

Isaac nods in compliance while Jane opens up the tray and impatiently sees what was on the menu for today.

She wifts the sweet smells of the sweet potatoes and slices of turkey on the plate, sided with green peas and caramelized carrots. She's anxious to eat as she grabs a plastic fork and starts to shuffle through the sweet potatoes. To savor every bite of real food she hasn't had in a very long time.

"Oh my!" she says as she savors her first bite. Every bit of sweet potatoes rolling around on her tongue.

"Oh yes!" she moans, feeling elated by the taste of turkey and enjoying the rough yet smooth texture of the meat.

"Hospital food can't be that good." Isaac says, admiring his daughter's hunger for food.

"When you haven't eaten in weeks Dad. Anything tastes good." Jane replies. She gulps down the turkey and mixes it in with the juices from the sweet potatoes. She forks through all of her food until her plate is wiped clean, turning her attention towards the cups of jello placed on the side of her tray.

Until another knock is heard at the door.

Instead of waiting for someone to answer, the doctor opens up and peeks through the door. He's delighted to see Jane's plate empty along with a healthy smile on her face. As she opens up the carton of Jell-O, she pauses for a moment to pay attention to the doctor and what he has to say.

He says, "Well don't stop for me. I can only imagine how you feel along with how your stomach feels. Especially after the ordeal you have been through, Ms. McKenzie."

She continues to listen to the doctor while peeling open the carton of Jell-O.

Isaac stares at the doctor with intent to hear what he has to say.

"Well. I'm just going to start by saying that Jane has made a remarkable recovery, physically and mentally from the trauma she has suffered over the past couple of weeks. They're very few patients that can recover back to normal at the speed she has had. After such a traumatic event. I just want to extend my help to you Jane and your family before you leave."

The doctor glances his eyes back and forth between Jane and Isaac.

"I only want to see you recover well and see that you have a happy, normal life after this."

The doctor hands her a card along with handing Isaac the same one and then steps out the door to leave them in peace.

Jane puts the card down to scrape the last bits of Jell-O that lie in the bottom of the plastic container.

After scraping the last bites of Jell-O and completely engorged in food, she says "Dad. I'm going to get changed so we can get out of here."

He looks up at her and complies. Eager to leave this place behind as well.

Jane moves slowly into the bathroom, feeling free from the IV yet delicate from losing the support of the pole. She puts on her clothes, throwing on her favorite shirt and sweatpants, feeling a sense of normality enter back into her body. She throws on some sneakers and her jacket ready to face the world again when she steps out of the bathroom. Her dad gets the queue that she's ready to go when she's halfway out of the door. He follows her swiftly to open the door as they both head out of the room.

She steps in the elevator and looks back at all of the nurses bustling around trying to do their jobs and takes a final farewell look at the hospital and staff before the elevator door closes.

Upon arrival to her home, she is impatient to step out and see her place of sanctuary. Going home was the first thing that came to her mind when she was running from her captives and when she woke up from her coma. A thought easily understood based on the circumstances she was in.

She steps out of the car to gaze her eyes across the brown sandstone of her home. Recognizing the set of stairs, she has walked across for many years and the rustic oak tree that stands present in front of her home.

Jane walks up the stairs and waits for her father to open the door after tipping the driver. Though once Jane steps into the house, her anticipation seized to the eerie quiet in the house. She senses a desolate presence looming through the walls that she has never felt before. Her home that was always bustling with people whenever she stepped through the door was now greeting her with silence and the dreary sounds of loss.

She looks around and can feel the tension circling in the air. An empty home, an absent mother, no remnants of a home that existed before she left for that party.

"Where's mom?" she says, eyeing every corner of the house in search for the life she once knew.

"She went to her mother's house in Colorado. She should be back in a few days."

"Why'd she leave?" Jane asks.

Isaac replies, feeling his body sink into the dining room chair, "Stress baby. This has been a lot on your mother and me."

Jane can see the exhaustion of the past months on Isaac's face, as tears begin to well into her eyes.

"I guess that's my fault." she says, holding back the tears of feeling like the victim and the perpetrator."

"Jane, only time and maybe God are to blame for these past couple of months. But don't burden yourself with the blame game. We can only move forward and grow stronger."

As Isaac tries to comfort her with his words, an unfortunate guilt plays in her mind as it plays within her heart.

She says, "Dad, I don't know. It doesn't feel like anyone's fault other than my own."

"Well don't feel that Jane." Isaac says in a louder tone. "You cannot blame yourself for these things. Don't try to guilt yourself."

She takes a deep breath before hugging her father and walking upstairs to go to her room. As she steps upon the second floor and looks over towards Marcus' room, she feels a call to open his door and see the remnants of what her brother left behind.

Though as soon as she opened the door, Jane falls to the ground as she looks upon a horrendous sight. Bewildered by the bare space that used to be Marcus' room, she screams to the top of her lungs and hysterically cries.

"What happened to his room?!" she cries aloud as she sits on the floor, letting hopelessness wash over her face. She feels in the pit of her chest, the weight of regret. That she shouldn't have even woke up from the coma or made it out of the storage container.

"Why?!" she yells. "Why? Why?!" Her cries bring footsteps up the stairs as they slow in pace behind her.

"This place is not my home anymore. I don't know this place."

Her Dad kneels behind her and gently pulls her closer. His comfort tries to soothe her as she releases her feelings onto the floor.

Isaac tries to stay strong for his daughter by fighting back his tears. He says "It's okay my love. Just let it out, I'm here."

Jane bellows out the ill feeling of waking up to her brother's death. She tries to release the burden but the pain only gets worse."

Isaac says, "I know you don't want to hear this but I have been beating this thought in my head. I found this encouraging phrase to say when things get low like this. That when everything in the world is telling you to stop and give up, know that everything changes so stop is never possible. In this world... good things come and bad things come as well. Everything interchanges and nothing stays the same forever."

"So, when does it stop?"

Jane says as her tears start to lighten up.

He says, "Know this Jane." As the tears he's been holding back start to flow from his eyes. "With change. You either let it take ahold of you and make you quit or you conquer it and see yourself rise."

With all the strength he has left within him, he looks his daughter in the eyes and says, "You conquer it and see where this change takes you. Because again, nothing stays the same."

Jane can feel her father's strength leave his body and transfer into hers. Isaac kisses her on her forehead as he sees her tears start to fade.

Jane hears.

You need to write Jane.

She embraces her dad for a few moments before walking towards the door.

"I think I'm going to get some rest." she says

Isaac gets up and says, "Okay baby, I understand."

Jane wipes the tears from his eyes.

Isaac says, "Do you mind leaving your door open? Just a precaution to all this mess that's been going on. Being alone sometimes, enclosed in your thoughts can be the worse for us right now."

Jane agrees and walks back into her room. She hears her Dad

start to break down again as he opens the box of Marcus' things and wallows in them. For her own sake, she tries to tune out his cries to prevent herself from starting up again.

Instead she walks to her desk and finds pieces of paper and a pen to write her feelings down.

She writes.

Everything changes. Nothing can stay the same,

Yet fear within change is always to blame.

Resistance only fuels in the crevices of doubt,

So, when uncertainty unveils. Do you choose to fade in or stand out?

Tears begins to fall from her eyes as she reminisces on the loss of her brother and her friend. She drifts to the memories within captivity and how that led to her 3-week coma. She cries silently over the past for a moment before cutting through that pent-up emotion, expressing through her words what she has been feeling. She tries to release them from her mind and her life as she writes every word.

"This feeling doesn't serve me anymore." she says. "Feeling the pain of the past won't turn back the hands of time. I've overcome a lot of things these past weeks. And if I can still stand after all of this. I can still stand."

You're strong Jane. You have a fierce power within you.

"I sure do." Jane agrees. As she turns her attention towards her parchment.

Sometimes a sad story is an only means to vent,

since you got to get what's hurting you off of your chest.

Sometimes you got to cry and hear your screams echo in the world,

And sometimes you got to ride those tears and feel them fall onto the Earth.

There's nothing wrong with you. You just do what you got to do,

Keep your strength in you. Vent away and let the repressed break through.

A hard lesson is a lesson learned through tears and feeling pain,

The beauty of life is you're always learning, so learn to live with no shame.

She takes one last glance at the parchment, noting the dried teardrops on the side of the page. Jane pushes away from her desk to go lay on her bed, feeling her mind clearer and some of the burden lifting off.

CHAPTER VII

Jane lies back in her bed and tries to relax her mind to sleep, ignoring the dulling throb that has been consistent in her head for the past couple of days since she's been back. She hears footsteps walk up the stairs towards her room and decides to look over while they open the door.

"How are those headaches doing?"

Jane begins to massage her head to ease the pain. She says, "Still the same. Being annoying."

"Maybe you should call the doctor." Isaac suggests. "It couldn't hurt, especially since they're not letting up."

Jane starts to shake her head and grunt. "Dad. I'm done with doctors for right now. This headache isn't anything that a little Tylenol couldn't fix."

Isaac adds, "Even though it's not fixing it."

"Your mother is coming home tomorrow." he says to her, thinking the news will make her feel better and deter her from the throbbing sensation in her head.

Although the news did deter her from her headache, hearing her mother coming home only worsened her mood.

"How is she doing?" she asks.

Isaac says, "She's doing okay. She got the time she needed."

"I need some of that time." Jane says.

"Yea we all need that time. Everybody needs time but we have each other to help and work through this together." Isaac replies.

He leaves her room, leaving her with her thoughts and throbbing headache. As Jane ponders the benefit of staying in a sad house.

"It's like I fall into a default mode every time I'm left alone. This mode of not knowing how to cover up this silence without doing something I once liked, but now resent. Since nothing can fill up the void."

"Nothing fills me but the pain of remorse."

Jane wants to cry but instead of wallowing in her agony, she gets up and stands in front of her mirror.

"Fade in or stand out, Jane? Fade into this shit or stand out."

She repeats the phrase in her mind as she remains looking at herself in the mirror. She sees a version of herself that she'd never thought she'd see. A person that went through the depths of fear, yet still managed to remain here. Alive.

Looking at her clock to check the time as she lays in her bed, she dreads the moments counting down to tomorrow. The showdown between her parents is not going to help. Her main focus is to heal and find sanity within her life again.

She decides to not concentrate on the problems in her life and concentrate on a solution to her biggest predicament; healing.

She moves away from her mirror and stares at the ceiling, finding comfort within her bed. She waits for an idea to pop into her head, but instead of coming up with a miraculous solution, she hears her phone jingle from her desk.

A text message from Tola:

Tola: Hey, Are you home?

Jane: Yea

Tola: Can I come see you?

Jane's eyes start to light up. As she may have found a solution to her problem

Jane: It's kind of late for that. Maybe tomorrow?

Tola: Yea. Sounds good to me.

Jane: I'll come your way. I need a break from being home.

Tola: Copy. Lmk when you're on your way.

Jane: ok

After days of moping around and crying, Jane's delightful smile starts to reappear on her face. She puts her phone down and now anticipates the counting down of the clock till tomorrow. She gazes out of the window and prepares for an adventurous day, brainstorming a means to escape her family and to finally have some peace of mind. Her eyes start to dim and close.

Waiting for tomorrow to come.

Waiting for a new day to begin.

Jane sees the light of the sun and gets out of bed as she feels a motivation to live the day. She starts to get ready for the day and walks to the bathroom to hop in the shower. Until she slows her pace, hearing her father talking to her mother.

She hears her father say, "Yea she's doing okay. Still suffering from headaches but doing okay."

She hears her father mention family counseling and rolls her eyes, anticipating the unveiling of time to the psychologist along with the emotions.

After hearing those words, she tunes her family out. Heading straight into the bathroom and feeling sure about her plan to get away.

She showers and lets the steam wash away the scars of the past. She hurries back into her room before her mother comes home. She searches through her closet for a duffel bag and packs it with her essential items of clothing, running back and forth into the bathroom to grab all of her toiletries and hair essentials.

She grabs her stack of allowance money with some pieces of parchment and pens. She stumbles across a jar in the bottom draw with remnants of herb in it. She thinks where she's going that she will need it, she packs it along with her stuff too and quickly moves to Marcus' room to drop the bag out of his window.

Q. IMAGINE

As she drops it carefully out of the window, it lands and hardly makes any noise at all. The success of her plan brings some life into her eyes as she lies on her bed and awaits the showdown.

An hour passes before she hears a knock on the door. Causing her to raise to her feet in an instant. Isaac opens the door without saying a word and swiftly embraces his wife with love. As Jane walks out of her room to see her family embracing down the stairs.

Billie looks up the stairs and turns her attention towards her daughter standing over the staircase. Jane gives her a dim smile as Billie gives her a heartfelt smile.

"Welcome home Jane!" she says as she lowers her bag on the floor. Billie opens her arms for an embrace as Jane slowly walks down the stairs.

"Welcome home to you." Jane says, trying to smile and look happy to see her as well. Billie opens her arm for a hug and embraces her daughter's small and frail body. She can feel her mother begin to choke up, only making her more adamant to leave.

"So, how are you?" Billie says to break up the silence. "I see you've gotten thin. Have you been eating?"

Jane says, "Yea I have. I guess that's what happens when you're asleep for a few weeks. Dad's been trying to cook but it's been mostly take out. That's never been an issue."

"How's grandma?" she asks.

Billie chuckles and says. "She's good. She's still being grandma, her wise and kooky self. She's concerned about you.

"I know. I'm concerned for me too."

Billie rubs her back to comfort her. "Well let's catch up. Tell me what's going on."

Jane takes a deep breath as she sits down at the dining room table with her family. She looks into her parent's caring eyes and can feel the need to run away.

She says, "Mom and Dad, I know you want to help and be there for me and I love you for that. But I feel like I'm drowning here, in this home, with all of these memories of the life I had but drastically died."

Billie jumps in. "Jane, it didn't die. Your still here so you have time."

Jane says, "Yea I know that. My brain knows that but it's not what I feel. I feel like I'm drowning the more I see these walls and your sad faces."

Isaac says, "Well that's why me and your mother have considered finding you a counselor, better yet a family counselor. We're all still grieving."

And in that moment, Jane unveils what has been contemplating in her mind.

"Okay but I need to put myself first on this. I can't be here in this house. I don't want to be here and I want to leave. I can't be here and I want to stay at a friend's house."

Isaac says, "Jane, I don't know about this. You just came back home and with all that happened, I don't feel comfortable with you leaving."

"Dad and Mom. All due respect but I don't feel like I'm even here now. I feel like I've been gone since the night of the party. I've faded away from this family and for me to come back, I need a break from this house and this sadness."

Billie says "Jane, I understand that you're hurt. But I cannot let you leave this house and go stay with another one's family. It would be the same thing and we want to be there for you."

Jane's anger starts to rise.

"So, I'm a prisoner. I was already shackled against my will and now I'm being held like a captive in my own home. You're not listening to me and I need you to listen because that'll help."

"Calm down Jane. Your mother is just worried." Isaac says.

"Well I'm worried too!" Jane yells. "I'm worried about my life and my sanity here. I can't even breathe here. My skin crawls as I walk through these hallways."

"Well Jane. You have to stay and fight this. This is your home. You can't run away when things start to get hard." Isaac says.

"Oh, you have a lot of nerve, telling me I can't run when both you have been running. You both have had breaks."

"Watch what you say Jane, because me leaving was not a vacation. I was hurt and overwhelmed..."

"Well, so have I?" Jane eyes widen in disbelief. "I'm the one that has been going through this. I'm the one in the mist while you all stand on the sidelines watching. Did you forget that? Did we all somehow forget that this is mostly my problem that you're helping me with."

The heaviness of Jane's words lay on their chest and minds as Billie's anger turns into a weeping submit. Billie wipes the tears and starts to gaze at her daughter. Feeling remorse.

"Jane. We're not perfect people."

Jane says, "I understand that and I don't expect you to be perfect. But I expect you to listen and take my opinion into consideration. I'm doing this for me. I need time to heal and feel better. Just for a couple of days and I'll let you know when I get there."

Tears start to fall from both of their eyes as they submit and allow her to leave.

"Just for a couple of days." Isaac says, as he tries to console his wife.

Jane walks away from the dining room table leaving her parents to their healing, quickly running into her room to catch a breath. To reprieve. To exhale.

Before she walks down to grab her coat, she sees an empty piece of loose leaf on her desk and feels the urge to write.

"One last vent before I leave."

> For the first time in my life, my mind hasn't been my friend,
>
> Fighting in this battle where my mind doesn't see an end.

Q. IMAGINE

The only time I feel sublime is when my mind drifts behind my eyes,

And all of the lies that drift in my mind, find a halt and the feelings subside.

The feelings don't die, All I do is cry,

I don't know about freedom because this life feels like a bind.

I'm tired of the woes of the world bludgeoning me at every turn,

Bashing me with hurt, running against the friction and feeling the burn,

I love my life but I'm tired of this fight,

I'm tired of feeling like this life has no light,

No beam of hope to shine out these fears,

No dreams of comfort to help this fog clear,

I am who I am and I can't fight how I feel,

If what I feel is fake, then I question what is real,

Why can't I feel love? I give but get nothing back,

All I get is some facts, of how this feeling will never last,

But when will it end?

Jane reads what she wrote and begins to ball into her hands. She says, "I'm going to find an end. Fade in or stand out."

As she wipes the tears falling from her eyes, she grabs her hat and coat to keep her warm from the cool breeze of fall. As she walks down the stairs to the side of her house and grabs her duffel bag, she begins to feel a glint of hope. An initial step towards becoming a girl that has lived and overcame.

As Jane walks down the block, she texts Tola to let him know she's on her way. She sees his building a few blocks away and looks forward to hanging out with him.

As his building approaches, she sees the young and handsome boy standing outside of his building with a rose in hand and a big gleeful smile.

He walks up to her and gives her a warming hug and says, "I see

Q. IMAGINE

you've gotten skinnier".

"Yea that's what happens when you sleep for 3 weeks. Can't eat and dream at the same time."

Jane says as she pulls away from him to see his face, "I really missed you."

Tola laughs and says, "Girl, don't go getting all mushy on me. Have my mind start fantasizing and stuff." He then looks at her duffel bag and says, "You're moving in or something?"

Jane chuckles and starts to scratch her head. "I mean if you don't mind. Just for a little while. I'm going through some things at home and I need to get away for a little."

Tola places his arm around her and leads her into his apartment. He says "C'mon in Jane. I see we have a lot to catch up on."

Tola opens up the door and swiftly leads her up the stairs towards his apartment. He unlocks the door and reveals his humble abode to her. It's relatively neat and spacious to her surprise that's filled with the scent of herb and an array of paraphernalia.

"Nice place you got here." she says.

"Yea hustling hard does that too you. It's the reason why I got to keep my clients happy and healthy. So, I can keep this place."

"Yea. Especially in Brooklyn." Jane adds.

She looks around and starts to absorb the minor details of his home. His living room hosting a large corduroy couch with an unplugged TV. A glass coffee table covered in ash and water pipes.

Jane sits down on his couch while he throws her bag into the bedroom and turns her attention towards the tapestry behind the couch and the tree of life symbolized on it.

"What a coincidence?" she says.

"I can turn the heat on if you get cold" he says to her as he walks back into the living room.

Jane smiles and walks past him to open her bag, reaching for her jar with the remnants of herb. She shows it to Tola as she passes by him again and says, "This should warm me up nicely."

He smiles and admires her spirit especially her fiery spirit and appetite for herb.

He says to her, "I don't think that herb I gave you is still good but we can try."

She says "Well my system is virgin right now so I don't think I need your super strength stuff right now. Got to ease into it."

Jane begins to throw the nugs of herb in the grinder to grind it up. As Tola grabs one of his water pipes off the table to clean it and fill it with water. She notices the view he has from his window and how she can see the Brooklyn bridge and Manhattann perfectly from his living room window.

"You must have quite the clients to have a view like this."

Tola laughs from the bathroom. "Jane, stop making me blush."

"Seriously", she says. "You can see everything from your window. All the sightseer tourist pay so much money to see. You should rent your view and charge a pretty penny for it."

Q. IMAGINE

Tola smiles gleefully as he walks out of the bathroom to put the water pipe on the table while Jane starts to pack it out.

"So, should I wait till a higher moment to ask what's happened or can I ask now?"

Jane fully packs the bowl and says, "Let's talk about it at a higher moment."

Jane lights the herb and fills up the glass with the milky white smoke. She inhales it all in and clears the pipe as if she never stopped smoking.

"Still a pro, I see" Tola says.

Jane exhales all of the smoke and creates a cloud. She doesn't choke or cough as she passes the water pipe to him.

"Some things you just don't forget."

They pass the water pipe until the bowl is kicked to which Jane gladly repacks it time after time. Tola cracks open up a window to release the cloud as he starts to light an incense. The aroma from the incense takes Jane back to the times smoking with all of her friends at Uncle Sook's. She smiles as she reminisces on the good times, she had with all of them. The good times she had high and the memories spent drifting on a cloud.

Silence starts to persist between them. Jane's mind drifts to her blissful memories while Tola drifts to Jane. He says, "So now that we're high. Please let me hear the story of your life this past month."

Jane half-wittedly smiles as she's caught up in a reminiscent moment.

She says to him, "Well I can really only tell you what happened the night of the party and the day after Joe's party. Along with what happened say...last week and a half. Everything else was when I was in a coma. Although I do recall what I experienced in my comatose state but we're definitely going to need to be higher for that."

"We'll that is a part of your story, right? No judgements here. I want to know." he says.

Tola perches up in his chair as he listens attentively to Jane's story. The bong passes between the both of them as Jane leans back and explains her life, starting with their evening walk and ending up at the point they are at right now.

As she explains her story, she begins to piece together the puzzle her life has been and Tola doesn't say a word. Just listens. He doesn't express any judgements on his face and simply nods to her once in a while to let her know he's still listening.

The herb in Jane's jar starts to finish which prompts Tola to take out his new stash and start to roll a canon for them. Jane continues to express her thoughts and experiences while he rolls the canon. She drifts to the emotional passages of her story as she feels a weight lifting off of her chest as she speaks every emotion or thought that crosses her mind. She gazes upon Tola as he listens to her.

No judgements.

No criticism.

Silence starts to take over the room when Jane finishes with her story. Tola lights the canon in silence while he processes everything she said. Her curiosity starts to intense as he lights the canon. Jane patiently waits to hear his thoughts.

Though silence still plagues the space between them, she decides to ask, "What do you think?"

Tola has an intense look on his face. Almost angry. He pulls smoke from the canon and French inhales it beautifully to calm his nerves. He takes a couple of more pulls before handing it to her and leans over to gaze deeply into her eyes.

He says, "You're an incredible woman, Jane."

Jane stares back, noticing a change in his emerald eyes as his eyes gleam brighter and clearer than they have before.

He says, "You might be the strongest woman I've ever met. And not a strong girl.... a strong woman. No girl could have gone through what you have in only a month and still be able to stand strong. To keep going. Fight off grown men while she's been chained and starved, breaking her wrist to get free. To confront death and the loss of her brother as well as confront the death of her friend. No girl and most woman could not mentally endure that and still stay so strong as you have Jane. You are truly a gift and I mean that."

Jane starts to blush so much; her cheeks start to hurt from the amount of smiling.

She says, "That means a lot Tola. You might be one of the first people who doesn't look at me like a victim."

He turns at her in confoundment. "Victim is the exact opposite of what you are Jane. Victims wouldn't have made it nearly as far as you have and conquered what you have. You're a hero."

Jane begins to blush as touching tears start to fall from her eyes.

She hits the cannon to calm her nerves and then hands it back to Tola. Admiring the sentimental words, he has caressed her ears with.

"I appreciate what you said to me. Even though I did have help from Alice to keep moving forward. Even to write more" she says.

"So, where'd you get the name Alice from?" he asks.

Jane says, "I don't know. That's the name I heard."

He says, "Are you sure you heard the name Alice?"

Jane stares at him and smiles realizing his intent. She says, "I'm positive. I heard the name Alice clearly in my room."

"Do you know anyone named Alice?" he asks trying to figure it out.

Jane starts to think as an Alice starts to cross her mind. "I mean….my middle name is Alice."

Tola laughs as Jane looks at him confused. "Well Jane. I guess you do take all of the credit for helping yourself out of your situation."

"What do you mean?" she says.

Tola says, "You heard of a higher conscious before?"

"Yea." she says.

"Well…that's Alice. You have been listening to yourself. That part of you that believes in living and finding happiness."

Jane says, "Well then how can my higher conscious know things about my life before it happened or warn me?"

"Because your higher consciousness saw the path and obstacles laid out that you created. Every action has a reaction. A part of you was just preparing yourself for an obstacle and showing you how your actions can change and create a new path. A better one."

Jane looks off into the distance as she processes certain things that Alice has said to her. She thinks of how Alice appeared when she started to question herself. Started to doubt herself.

"Wow" she says. "I really didn't know who that was but....... I knew it was something within me. I thought I was going crazy."

Tola says, "Everyone has a conscious. That aspect of themselves that guides them towards their path or a better path. I know because I haven't had it easy either. I needed some encouragement to keep on going when I was living on the street. There was a time I thought about giving it all up. Just being done and free of this burden called life. But I felt something keeping me going. Giving me signs and whispering in my ear that things will get better. That this point of my life is only a transition making me stronger and preparing me for the next step in my life."

Jane moves in closer to Tola as she rests her head on his chest. She feels a warmth in her chest while gazing into Tola's eyes and listening to his heartbeat.

He says, "I listened like you did Jane and it got me to this point I am right now. Now, I'm happy. I found my happy place."

Jane is taken over with the kindredness she feels for Tola. She leans in and kisses him gently, feeling the warmth and loving spirit within him as their lips touch. The softness of his lips.

The gentleness in his hands as he caresses her face, kissing her passionately.

Both are encompassed with intense feelings felt between them. The emotions run high as Jane stands up and takes Tola's hand to lead him into the bedroom. She stands on the side of the bed and stares at the distant wall of his bedroom. Until she feels Tola push up against her from behind as he gently brushes away her hair to kiss her on her neck. Jane pushes her body close to his as she feels the magic between them intensify and spark.

Jane removes her shirt and removes his in the process. Leaning back on the bed to watch Tola run his lips all over her body. She lays back and relaxes feeling a sensation, she hasn't felt in a long time. A feeling she has been searching for in her home but found it in the heart of Tola.

Love.

CHAPTER VIII

Jane opens her eyes and feels exuberant. Her eyes drift over to Tola as she sees him peacefully sleeping and wrapping her in her arms. She manages to slip through his grasp and run to the bathroom noticing a glow radiating from her face as she looks into the mirror. She smiles and laughs as she reminisces on the events of last night. The heights that Tola and her reached together with the love they made. She sniffs his shirt and breathes in his scent, enjoying the beautiful feeling she has floating in her chest.

Jane leaves the bathroom to grab a piece of parchment and pen from her bag. Tip toeing into the living room and starting to write.

> Love
>
> What is "love"?
>
> Is love the airy feeling in your chest when you can't stop thinking about someone?
>
> That one person who excited and inspired the thought of love's existence?

A thought that you. Of all people are experiencing this blissful feeling.

Love to me is so deep and so powerful, I am almost afraid of feeling it.

To be that bonded with a person that all they have to do is exist and that's okay.

That's all you need from them. Is to exist and be.

Whatever they desire.

Whomever they want to be.

To have the mind to appreciate and accept a boundless love.

To be completely one with and have our spirits intertwined.

To the point where we can be apart and the love will still blossom.

Our bodies can stray away from each other and the

spark will still prevail.

Love.

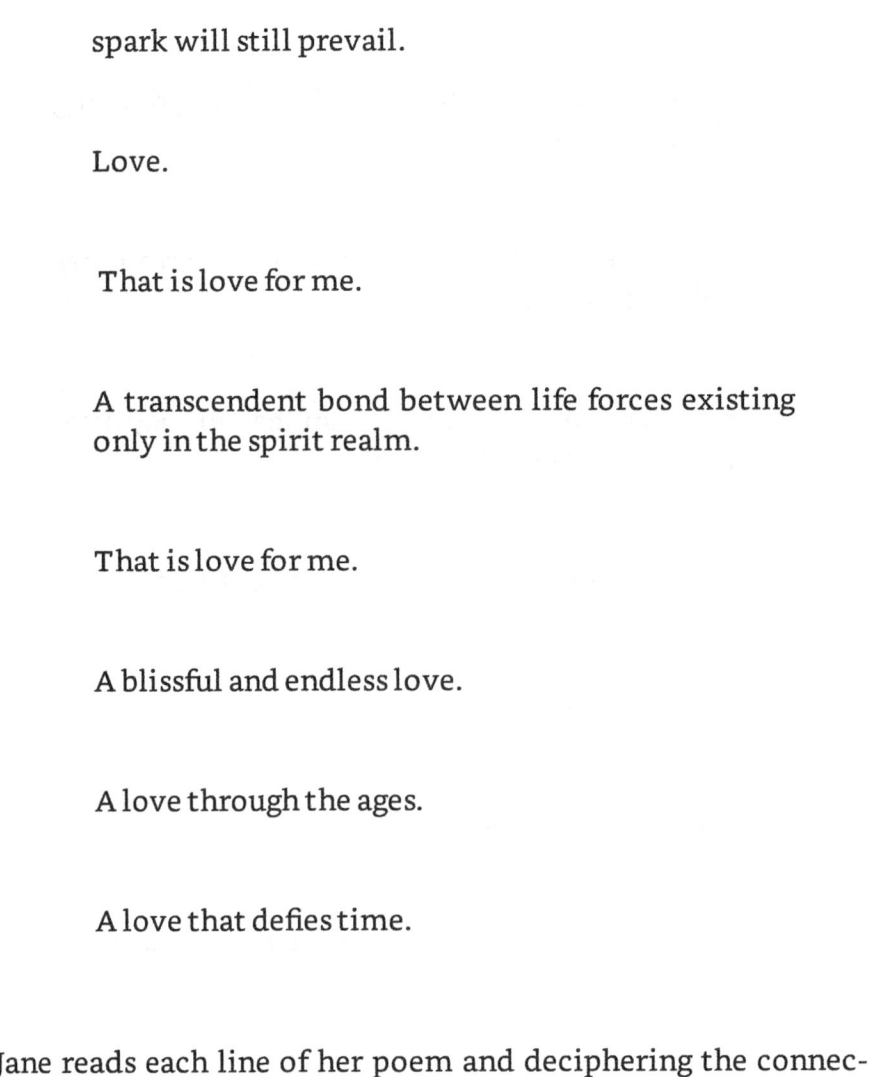

That is love for me.

A transcendent bond between life forces existing only in the spirit realm.

That is love for me.

A blissful and endless love.

A love through the ages.

A love that defies time.

Jane reads each line of her poem and deciphering the connection between her and Tola.

"I don't know if we're there yet but the future is always prosperous."

She folds up the poem and heads back to the bed, hearing Tola shuffle in his bed searching for Jane's warmth.

She quickly hops back into bed and starts playing in his long blonde locks.

"How are you awake at this moment?" he mumbles to her.

She leans in and kisses him on his cheek. "I was inspired. My mind was calling me to write. Couldn't fight the force."

Tola moves his body closer to her and starts to nuzzle his nose on her neck. "You're too warm to be leaving this bed right now."

She leans in and kisses him on his nose, sparking his eyes to open up.

"Can I roll a joint?" she asks.

"You're asking me to roll a joint? Wake and bake is the best way to start a day" he says.

Jane jumps out of bed and walks towards the living room. Noticing there's no more herb on the coffee table, she yells towards the bedroom "Where's your stash?"

Slowly but surely, he replies "Just pick one off of the tree in the room behind the TV."

"Pick one off of the tree?" Jane re utters to herself.

Excited to see what else Tola has in store in this hidden backroom, she opens the door and her nose is instantly hit with the smell of herb. The room is dark but dimly lit by a red glow. Her eyes are hit with the sight of a few a large bushes. In resemblance to Christmas trees. The aroma and color from the plant ignited Jane as she gazes upon the plant.

"So, this is what it looks like?"

She starts to analyze the tree, noting the various amount of buds covering the evergreen leaves.

"I almost don't want to pick one. It's too beautiful."

Jane searches around the tree and finds one nug slightly hanging off more than the others. She grabs it and gently breaks it off of the plant, gazing up at all of the magnificent trees growing in this dark room. She walks out of the room and into the living room. She grabs some rolling paper and a grinder to light. As she heads back into the bedroom, Tola is up and sitting perched in his bed. Awaiting Jane's arrival.

"So, what do you think about my women?" he asks.

Jane smiles and walks to her side of the bed. She says, "They're beautiful. I almost didn't want to take a nug."

Tola laughs and notices the nug she pulled. "Yea I feel you. I love them. Starting to grow my own instead of buying from other growers."

He grabs her hand to glance at the nug and say, "The one you picked is definitely one of my favorites. She's a twin to the other plant I harvested and smoked. That's the one I sold to you last month."

Jane smiles and feels her cheeks start to rosy up. "So, I get special privileges?" she asks.

"Yea that's what I wanted to talk about with you Jane." he says. "I really like you Jane. I don't want to move too fast but…."

Jane pushes her finger to his lips and says, "Then let's not. Let's just live for right now and enjoy what we share in this instance."

She moves her hand and starts to grind up the nug. "If we get to that point, I think you're talking about, then that's beautiful. But I don't want to jump. I just want to live this moment. I haven't had a good moment like this in a while and I just want to cherish it especially since it's with you."

Tola stares at her passionately as he watches her pack the rolling paper and start to roll. He blurts out, "I get that and you're right. Let's just see how it goes."

Jane finishes rolling the joint and begins to spark it. Once she passes it to him, she asks "I can still crash for a little while right?"

Tola smiles and says, "Got to keep wooing you right?"

Jane laughs as she watches him hit the joint and French inhale it. "Guess so. I'm going to view you as my doctor. Giving me doses of herb and treating me with love."

Tola takes another hit as he starts to smile and giggle. "Call me Dr. T. Serving up T-Time for my patients."

They both start to laugh with delight as the joint passes in between the both of them. Tola plays some reggae to keep the spirits lifted as they smoke and talk. Their eyes fading back as Tola rolls another joint.

Until their sweet dreams and comfort are interrupted by the sudden ringing of Jane's phone. They both stir in bed as they try to figure out whose phone is it, finding her phone on the ground and picking it up without looking at the ID.

"Hello." she says.

"Baby girl, where are you?" Isaac asks concerned.

Jane's eyes widen as she realizes it's her father. She says, "I'm at a friend's house."

"You didn't text me to let me know. Which friend's house are you staying at?" he asks.

Jane hesitates to answer truthfully.

She says, "Dad. I'm at Tola's house." Immediately regretting the decision to confess.

"Tola?! Who the hell is Tola?"

Jane can hear his temper raise from a concerned parent to an angry one.

"We've been friends for a while. I'm staying with him until I feel I can come home "she says.

"Oh, hell no Jane. Bring your butt home now."

"What? You said I can stay a couple of days."

"Well me and your mother talked about this after you left. We want to work on our relationship as a family and work with you through this. We need you home, especially since you're staying with some boy."

Jane's calm but coy demeanor turns into a fit of rage. She says adamantly, "Okay, that's sounds good for you. But what about me? What about what I need?"

Isaac tries to reason. "Jane. You need to come home. You need us as much as we need you. That's what we all need to do. To be a family. Together. In the same household."

"No, that's what you need!" she yells. "I'm not leaving yet. I just need some more space. I can't be around."

Isaac interrupts, "Jane I know you're upset and this has been a lot for you but think about someone other than yourself right now. Think about us as a whole."

"No!" she yells back. "I'm the only person thinking of me right now and I need time away. I need this. Why are you doing this to me?"

Isaac's tone changes. "I'm not doing anything to you! I'm looking out for you and our family. Please come home Jane or tell me where you are so I can pick you up."

You know what Dad." Jane looks at Tola confident in the words she's about to say. "I'm going to stay right here. I'm not leaving yet. Give me a couple of more days. Please?!"

"Excuse me?! he yells. "I said come home Jane. Now!"

She looks at her phone and contemplates her decision. Before saying to her father. "I'll come home. I'll see you in a few days."

Jane hangs up the phone and sees Tola listening in on the conversation. He looks a little uneased by the conversation he just overheard.

"Are you okay?" he asks.

Jane shouts "I get one moment of happiness and someone tries to ruin it."

Tola scoots his body towards her and starts to rub on her back. "Babe everyone has their ups and downs. They're your parents.

It's probably unintentional."

She leans her head on his shoulder to calm her nerves and her worries. "And I'm supposed to go back to school next week and try and finish up my last year. I don't know what I'm going to do. There's just too much going on. How can I try and focus?"

Tola looks at her and says, "What are you talking about Jane? You're going back to school and finishing up your last year. Don't let this beat you. It's your last year and you're already set for NYU. All you have to do is finish and graduate."

Jane starts to tear up as she kisses him on the lips. He wipes her tears away and kisses her on her cheek.

"Don't let this beat you. Or let anything stop you from living your dreams. Be whoever you want to be. Whatever is going to make you happy. And that's it."

Jane breaths out the tension in her heart as she turns to her pen and parchment to release what's left of the angst. She hears the phone ring in the background but ignores it and starts to write next to Tola.

> My heart's heavy, the world's weighing me down,
>
> Everybody wants to turn a smile into a frown.
>
> But why? Why do people have to be this way?

All I want to feel is peace but all I feel is dismay.

Is it me preventing this. Or Is it we?

Is it a groups effort keeping me trapped and my soul unfree?

I just want to feel…. positivity.

But you have to understand pain in order to know how to feel serenity.

But that is the end for me.

The end of analyzing myself until there's nothing left.

 The end of running through my thoughts until I can't catch a breath,

Feeling that I'm cursed or I'm not good enough.

Because it's these negative thoughts that brought me to this rut.

Q. IMAGINE

Jane takes a deep breath after she feels her heart lifting out of the bind it was just put in. She folds up her parchment and puts it back into her bag.

"Why do you always fold it up?" he asks.

"I don't know." she says. "My poems are my private thoughts. Something that is more therapeutic than smoking."

Tola says, "We'll let me hear one that's not so therapeutic. Or one that you would like to share."

Jane whips out her phone to search through the various documents in her notes.

Her eyes start to glint as he grins at one of them, she wrote a few years back.

"I called this one 'I just don't understand'."

Tola laughs and says, "I can only imagine what you question in this world."

Jane laughs and says, "Yes. I wrote this during my younger teenage years. Before I started smoking and couldn't suppress all of those angsty emotions building up."

"I can't wait to hear it." He says as Jane pulls up the file.

Jane starts to read it.

> Oh man, I just don't understand,

How people could be so spiteful and disconnected.
Are we still human?

Tola's eyes widen. "Damn, that's how you start it?"

She mildly shrugs her shoulder and begins to laugh. "I told you I was angsty. That's only the first stanza."

"Okay give it to me more."

I just don't understand. Our theories on our future,

Our scruples to make peace but beliefs that war is a solution.

I just don't understand.

How the bad is more possible than the creation of good,

We know how to progress in life but we don't think we should.

We know how to change our world but we don't think we could.

These thoughts just weigh us down because we

misunderstood.

How?

How can we be so blind?

How could we be so naive and imperceptive of our minds.

The fact that everything we made, we thought into creation,

But we can't think ourselves out of this self damnation.

I just don't understand.

The smartest species in the world can't even get it together,

But the opposite can thrive and probably live forever.

There's billions of us and we don't know how to share,

We'll rape and pollute the earth, don't even dare to care.

Acknowledging a spectacle but ignoring the reason,

Perceiving that our future is nothing good to believe in.

We band against each other and divide by traits,

Separate and separate until we're all displaced.

The consequence of man, we just don't understand.

We just don't understand that all we need is love,

Not hatred, not disdain, but an understanding of One.

One world. One race. No separations or divides,

Showing compassion for the differences we experience in life.

We are all a product of the environment we were

raised in,

And we all have no right to judge since we're all raised in sin.

Understanding the lessons learned as life changes and grows,

Knowing everyone has their path but you're unique to your own.

Understanding both sides can show the bigger picture,

To look from more than one lense even if it differs.

We are an expression of the soul created for the divine,

So don't be blinded by your mind and see beyond your eyes.

We're present on this earth for more than just our amusement,

We have a gift within us and we need to use it.

Not rest on our laurels or divert by choice,

We need to change and save our home while we still have a voice.

The prospect of man. Even though we don't understand,

We still have a chance.

Rubbing his chin, Tola stares into the distance in silence for a few minutes. He looks at her, pondering the words of her poem and what she's trying to say.

Jane watches him process the poem she wrote and after a few more minutes of Tola's silence, she asks "What do you think?"

"That's bars babe." he says to her still rubbing his chin. "I'm just surprised you said that was one of your older poems. What teenager sees all that?"

Jane shrugs again feeling more confident in her work and her style. "I don't know. Maybe I'm an old soul or just observant."

"Well you definitely don't see the world through rose colored glasses. But I like your viewpoint. At first I thought you were going too deep and view the world so negatively. But at the end, you changed it around and presented hope. I like that. You showed the negative but presented how the good can triumph."

Jane leans back on Tola and enjoys the beautiful comments he gives her.

"You know. I'm never going to leave if you keep complimenting me like this."

He laughs as she says, "Thank you."

Tola and Jane lay together in bliss and appreciation. Until their appreciation of each other turns into affection and they begin to make love.

Once their young bodies tire out and exhaust all emotion and energy, they lay in each other's arm and enjoy the feeling of one another until they drift away into their dreams.

CHAPTER IX

Drifting into the dream world feeling their minds leave their physical plane and travel into the infinity. Jane finds herself surrounded by the stars. She hears the voice of Alice in this space of light and wonder.

So you found your stone.

Jane looks around and sees a bright gleaming star shining at her.

She answers, "I don't have a stone."

What about the stone given to you? While you were in the coma. Where is that stone?

Jane answers, "I don't know. It wasn't my stone. It belonged to Sally."

And yet, who made Sally. Was it not you that wrote that story?

Jane says as she looks at her empty hands. "I don't have the stone."

You have it Jane. What did you tell Sally when you were in the realm of creation?

Jane thinks, "I told her that the stone is a representation of what she thought her soul was before. That she needed time to be alone in order to learn to love herself."

Yes and once she loved herself, she had enough love to give others. Correct?

Jane nods her head and agrees.

So that is you Jane. That is your story. You were Sally.

"How did I become something that I created?" Jane asks.

Because you created it. You were once lost in this world growing cold, were you not? Staying lost within your thoughts and taking things for granted. That is why you had to go through what you did. To learn. To feel and experience life. Even the bad parts.

Jane's eyes widen as she can feel a radiant glow radiate around her and flow throughout her body.

Jane, you have exceeded. And you will reap the benefits of keeping your strength and staying bright. But there are two things that I ask of you.

"Okay. What are they?"

First, you must rekindle with your parents. No one is perfect in this world and you cannot blame people for their imperfections. Perfection is only held in the realms of the infinite and not the ones of men. Rekindle and set your spirit free of this weight.

The words of Alice start to finally sink into Jane's mind as she feels gratitude for the help that has been given to her. She nods her head and says yes as she continues to listen to what she has to say.

Second, give away your stone. Although you think you don't have it since it is not in your hands. It is held within your heart and your mind. You can give your stone away by transforming. Become your dreams and spreading your love throughout the world. Sharing and strengthening people with your knowledge. That is the way. The motion of love.

Jane smiles as she feels the tasks that are required of her are the tasks she has always desired to perform. To feel happiness and be happy are the things Alice requires of her which fills her up with bliss and excitement.

"Thank you Alice. For everything. But before this ends, Can I ask one question of you?"

Ask away. We only have now.

"Who are you? or What are you?"

Oh Jane. They call me by many names and I answer and speak through all of them. I am within you. I guide you. Stay strong within love. Stay in the light.

Jane eyes flash from the bright luminescent of a star to the sight of a beach similar to the one she saw in the blank canvas. She feels the sand crawl between her toes as she walks down the shoreline and reminisces on the last beach scene she saw within her mind.

Jane walks down the shoreline and feels the warm water brush up against her feet. Looking on at the never ending shoreline and watching the string of clouds flow towards the beach. But to her surprise, she hears laughter. She looks further down the shoreline and sees figures embracing each other as they watch the sunset.

She moves closer to see who these figures are. Hearing voices that spark her memory but feeling unable to match them to a face.

Though her sight blurs the ability to recognize their faces, she continues to move forward. Feeling as if a force is pulling her towards these two people, she moves close enough to see their faces gaze upon the bliss that is held within their smiles. But her body compels her to keep a distance and observe from afar.

Jane catches her heart before it drifts out of her chest. Halting in her steps as she sees the gleeful spirits of her brother and her friend.

She watches their beautiful and innocent love transform from realm to realm, holding the zany and adventurous infatuation Marcus held for his first love and the erotic, sensual nature that Neal felt for his last.

Tears fall from her face as she feels the passion encapsulated in their bond. She sits on the sand and watches the beautiful site or her two loved ones at peace.

Not an inch of remorse of their faces.

Not a glimmer of regret within their smiles.

Jane's gratitude for this moment soars throughout her eyes, witnessing this flicker of the infinite and how love holds no boundaries. This farewell to the love she thought she lost was replenished with the knowledge that love only transforms.

She recognizes the benevolence in changes and challenges and understanding the meaning, 'things happen for a reason.'

"Wish me luck you too." she says as she continues to watch them on the beach.

She says "I have my own love to catch", before opening her eyes to the sight of Tola.

CHAPTER X

The moment Jane's eyes open, she feels as if she has awoken into a new world. Bursts of energy radiates through her body as she feels alive and awake.

She feels the past evaporate from her mind as the prospects of the now and future take control. Jane pushes Tola off of her and starts to jot down everything that Alice told her in her dreams, grabbing a sheet of parchment out of her bag and solidifying the requests. Though she feels hesitant about mending the relationship with her family, she wants to listen to Alice and understand why this has to be done.

"All they've given me was grief but I need to forgive the past to move on."

She starts to meditate on the past and how she felt ignored and neglected. Feeling resentment towards the both of them for not helping Marcus out and not understanding her. But then she hears.

They're human Jane. Nobody's perfect.

She starts to place her mind into the perspective of what she needs to gain from this, starting to reflect on all of the mistakes she's made and her imperfections.

"I really can't judge them. I've made more mistakes in my short life than they probably ever have.

Good things can come out of dark places Jane. Like a white flower hidden in a cave. It's obscured and blinded by its surroundings until someone searches through the dark and finds it standing out. That one flower you stumbled on could be the only thing that matters. The one positive rooted in a negative. So do not dwell on the cave and the bad or negative. Take the flowers and leave. Maybe you just needed a bouquet.

Jane takes a deep breath from the pit of her chest and forces all of the air in her lungs out of her chest. As she exhales, she feels the heavy weight of guilt lighten off of her chest. Each breath she takes makes her chest a little lighter. Her mind a little stronger.

"These weeks have been one hell of a ride." she says. "My life is literally a roller coaster."

"But like a rollercoaster, it has its ups and downs. It's parts where it takes you for a loop or a part where you have to go back in time and relive something. But it is one adventurous ride and it's my ride so I'm going to enjoy it."

She lays back in bed after placing the parchment down back in her bag, watching Tola sleep peacefully next to her until she gets the urge to grab her phone and walk into the living room.

Her phone starts to ring as she calls her father. Awaiting to hear the voice on the other line but prepares what she is going to say when he picks up. She hears Isaac say "hello" which gives her the go ahead to start off her reconciliation with him.

Tola can hear Jane talking from the living room as she makes amends with her parents. After ending the call, she walks back into the bedroom and is surprised to see Tola up and rolling.

"There you go with that morning bird mess." he says.

He watches Jane fill her duffel bag with clothes as he says. "Honeymoon's over I guess".

Jane laughs and hops on top of him, kissing him all over his face. "The honeymoon has just begun and this is the process."

She jumps back off of him to finish packing. As Tola ponders the meaning of her words. "How is your departure the start of the process of the honeymoon phase?"

She through all of her stuff in her bag as she says, "Because this is the moment we can be in love without getting on each other's nerves."

Jane smiles and gives him a gentle kiss on his lips before walking out of the bedroom. She says. "Told you it was temporary. I'll text you when I'm home."

Although Jane pretends not to hear the soft, faint voice of Tola whispering "Man, I love that girl." She ultimately starts to blush as she opens the front door and leaves the apartment.

Walking home to her house feels like the day she bumped into that guy on the sidewalk. It's just a beautiful fall day. The leaves have turned and the colorful array of fall leaves hover over the pavement and drift into the sky. She can't help but become mesmerized into the beauty of the trees as she walks down the sidewalk towards her home. She starts to say the words "Today is a good day." but she holds back. Instead she thinks of saying "I'm really enjoying this" but instead she says, "Thank you."

Thank you to whomever gave her this moment to enjoy. Led

her down this path to find this feeling. She thinks of Alice. She thinks of her family and friends. And she thinks of herself, who had the strength to overcome this.

CHAPTER XI

Months have passed since Jane overcame her challenges as it is now the end of the school year. One day before graduation. Jane looks at herself in the mirror, noticing the vibrancy in her skin and life in her eyes. She stands proud in her mirror, looking at the girl who managed to finish her senior year and prepare for her freshman year at NYU. She admires herself in the cap and gown for school, loving the crimson red gown on her skin and the crimson/black cap that fits half-heartedly on her curls.

"I made it." she says to herself.

Billie starts to call her down stairs for breakfast as Jane quickly removes her cap and gown to run downstairs for breakfast.

The smell of freshly made waffles and crisp bacon ruminates through the hallways and stairs. Greeting Jane's nose as she opens her bedroom door. Her mouth starts to water as the aroma gets stronger. Watching her mom finish up the waffle batter sets her dad sets the table. Jane walks to the corner table and passes a picture of Marcus places on the table. Before walking to the stove top and preparing her plate.

"Mom, this smells amazing. What type of waffles did you make?" Jane asks.

"These are maple buttermilk pancakes that I whipped up." Billie responds. She takes the last of the waffles out of the waffle maker and says, "I used some of that maple butter I bought from the supermarket and mixed with the buttermilk so...."

"You might not need to put any butter on those waffles." Isaac says as he chimes in.

Jane giggles and steps up to the counter to grab some of the sweet-smelling waffles along with some strips of crisp bacon. She pours some hot maple syrup on the waffles before sitting back down at the corner table and starts to dig in, enjoying every bite she takes. The warm waffles melt in her mouth as she sinks her teeth into then and enjoying the milky sweet taste they hold. The crisp crust mixed with the fluffy and buoyant middle makes the waffles superb. Mixing the sweet flavor with the salty, crisp bacon brings her taste buds to a state of bliss.

"This is amazing Mom." Jane says as she embraces the food. Billie smiles with delight as they all share their meal with laughter and jokes about past events and what has happened. Reminiscing on the good times of the past and not dwelling on the bad. They move on to a better place within their mind and feel happier since their family made it through a difficult time and still stayed together.

Jane looks at her phone and sees she only has a few more moments till school starts. She says, "Time for me to go." after eating the last of the food on her plate before walking to get her coat.

"Isn't this your last day." Billie says.

Jane nods her head in agreement as she places her plate in the sink. Before Jane can leave the kitchen, she feels her mother pull her close to her chest. Billie gives her a warming hug saying, "I'm so proud of you."

Jane embraces her back and starts to clench her mother tightly. Before letting go, Jane says, "Thank you." and goes to hug her father.

Outside of the house, Jane walks towards an Uber to take her to school. She steps inside and looks back at her house. Thinking about how good this morning felt and how she feels nothing but opportunity and fun for her last day of class.

The car pulls up in front of the school and Jane sees all of her friends waiting in front of the old Victorian building. She waves to Marcus' old friends before walking to her group.

"I see you're still taking Uber." Roscoe says as she walks up to them.

"Yea. The family wants me to feel safe after all of that. Plus……they want me to ride in style." Jane flips her hair and winks at Roscoe with a smile.

Lianne says, "That's my girl!"

Joe walks over in his letter head jacket and says, "You look amazing Jane…. truly. Glad you could finish up and graduate on time."

Jane smiles at Neal and says thank you, but she sees Lianne's disapproving look so she cuts the conversation short.

"Glad everything worked out with you too Joe. Can't wait to watch you on ESPN score your touchdowns."

Joe smiles and starts to blush before looking at Lianne's face and feeling the need to leave. She made no eye contact with him and either looked down or away from him but you could feel the anger she holds towards him even if her face was completely obscured.

Before Joe leaves, he says, "Well...I'll see you guys later then. Hopefully our last day will be a good one. Especially since we don't have to go to class."

Joe backs away and hopes Lianne will pass him a look before he turns him back. Instead she closes the circle where he once was and starts to talk to Jane.

"So. y'all ready to start the day?" she says.

Feeling Lianne trying to change the subject away from Joe, Jane presses the issue.

"Still mad at him I see."

Lianne starts to rub her head and feels her face getting flustered at the thought of him. "Not mad. Just done. He tried to talk to me after the party and I flipped out. I don't know why he can't get the hint."

Jane leans in and gives her a hug. "I think you need to talk to him. You can't let things end on a bad note like this. You don't want to start a new beginning with grudges from the past."

"Mmmm......speak that true knowledge Jane." Roscoe says.

They all laugh and start to head into the gymnasium where all the seniors are. "It's the last day and you might not see him again. You should really mend the broken ties."

Jane wraps her arm around Lianne and tries to cheer her up. It's the last day of school and it's a beautiful day in spring so she wants all of her friends to enjoy it.

Roscoe, Lianne and Jane sit on one of top bleachers in the large gymnasium. They sit and look at all of the activities presented for the seniors as well as the lineup of food stands against the far wall. From hot dogs and pizza to fried Oreos and ice cream, the student's mouths start to water by the sight and smells of the food. Scattered around the center of the gym are game stations like riding a bull, dodgeball, tug-of-war and a bouncy house obstacle course which every student is prepared to try first.

The gym teacher dressed in a red sweat suit with the school logo plastered in his breast, says "Okay Class of '17. You've all worked hard and today is the day you get to let loose. Remember the school rules but enjoy yourself."

He starts to blow his whistle before heading to his office in the men's locker room and the students race off the of the stairs and explore this mini carnival in front of them. Roscoe pulls out some brownies and shows them to Lianne and Jane before they step off of the bleachers.

"How about we spice it up a little bit?" he says.

Jane looks at the brownies and shakes her head no, surprising both Lianne and Roscoe.

She says before walking down, "I want to remember today."

Roscoe and Lianne split one brownie before meeting Jane at the mechanical bull station.

Jane steps up through the inflated outer rim of the mechanical bull. The guy instructs her to hold on for as long as she can and keep one hand up at all times.

"You get two turns." he says.

Jane steps up on the bull as her friends cheer her on. She hears the music start and a loud buzz before the bull starts to move and jerk around furiously in a circle. It spins around veraciously and then turns the other direction to get her to fall off but Jane stays strong for the first few minutes. With Roscoe and Lianne still cheering her on, she starts to wave to them when the bull starts to spin and jerk to loosen her grip. She flies off and hits the edge on the inflated barrier. Laughing as she stands up, she quickly hops back on for another try as the other senior's crowd around to see how long she lasts and give it a try after her.

The second time, she doesn't last as long since her legs get tired of holding such a strong grip. She flies off again within a few minutes and starts to head to some of the food courts to regain her energy.

First stop is the hot dog stand where the line is a little shorter than the one for the pizza. As their waiting in line, Jane sees Monica Gonzalez waiting on the same line a few steps ahead of her. Jane asks Roscoe to hold her spot as she runs to the bleachers to grab something out of her bag. When she walks back towards the line, she passes her friends and stands next to Monica.

"Hey. How's it going?" Jane says to her.

Surprised since her and Jane never spoke much during school, she says "Not bad. Not terrible for the last day of school."

Jane laughs and says, "Yea, especially with all of these activities and food stands around. Everything is free."

Monica smiles as she turns her attention away from Jane. "Free is always good."

Then Jane says, "Did you happen to write your speech yet for graduation? I know you probably did but is there any way you could include this into it. Maybe towards the end?"

Jane hands her a folded piece of paper which Monica is suspicious to take.

"It's something I wrote dedicated to my brother and Neal along with some stuff that I was going through earlier this year. You don't have to say I wrote it. I just.... would like you to share it to the class as a dedication to the students we lost this year."

Monica looks at the note and reads some of it. They shared the same creative writing class this year so she knows her writing isn't half bad. As she reads what's on the loose leaf, her eyes widen and she looks at Jane impressed by what she read.

"I think this would work out beautifully in my speech. I was going to dedicate a moment of the speech to Neal but didn't know where to put in into my speech. Thanks Jane. Can't wait to read your work someday."

Jane smiles at her and back away to go to her spot in the line. "Same goes to you Monica. I wish you the best in life.

Jane turns away with a gleam of excitement in her eye. She wasn't sure if Monica would agree even though she hoped she did.

Standing back in her spot with a gleaming smile on her face, Lianne asks "What was that?"

Jane looks in her direction with that same gleaming smile and says, "You'll see tomorrow."

Jane, Roscoe and Lianne make this plan to hit each one of the carts up to make in order to create a smorgasbord of food. The brownie kicked in for Lianne and Roscoe so they needed to hide away from any of the teachers and make sure they had a lot of food. Each one of them rounded up three of each and moved to the top of bleachers were the teachers couldn't see their faces as much. Roscoe came back with three tacos and three chalupas for the group. Jane brought the pizza and more hot dogs while Lianne brought the churros and a bucket of fried Oreos. Jane being the only sober person ate the food slow while the other two scarfed the food down like starving animals. You could see the satisfaction on their faces as they bite into their food and taste every morsel that went into it. Jane watched in admiration, wondering if that's how she looked when she was high with the munchies.

"Save one of the chalupas for me." she says as she notices there's only one left. They both start to laugh since they notice how fast they ate all of the food they just got.

"Sorry, girl. But I didn't have breakfast this morning and this brownie makes everything taste so good."

Jane laughs as she grabs the last chalupa, seeing Roscoe eyeing it and her. "Enjoy yourself. I'm just glad you're having a good time."

Roscoe finishes his chalupa and says, "You know. This is the most positive I've ever seen you Jane. Did you sleep over Tola's house last night or something?"

Jane starts to blush and throws an empty taco wrapper at Roscoe. She says, "No. I just had a good morning with my family.

Mom made a really good breakfast and we talked most of the morning instead of ignoring each other. It was really good."

Lianne jumps in and says, "Do you miss Marcus?"

Jane sighs as her smiling face starts to dim. "I miss him every day. The house feels better but I would rather have the silence than not have him. I really do regret not building a better relationship with him but...there's nothing I can do about that now."

Jane starts to wipe tears from her eyes. "I just have to move on and do my part helping kids like him who are going through a tough time."

"How are you going to do that?" Roscoe asks.

Jane's tears dry up and she smiles and says, "I guess you'll see tomorrow."

Lianne and Roscoe smile back at her and start to lean in and give her a hug. There embrace catches the attention of Joe and he starts to walk up the bleachers to join the group.

"Hey. What's going on here?" he says.

Lianne rolls her eyes. "None of your business Joe. Go away."

Joe steps closer and says, "No. I'm not going to go away until you talk to me."

Lianne looks at him and rolls her eyes again before standing up and walking across the bleachers with him to have some privacy and talk.

Jane and Roscoe look over and watch them duke it out for a

while before turning their attention back to the food that's left.

"Do you have any herb on you Roscoe?" she asks as she bites into a fried Oreo.

Roscoe starts to smirk and opens his bag to show her the fresh bag of herb he picked up.

Jane starts to smile as her mind drifts to the idea of having a farewell toke for Neal.

"How does a memorial toke at Uncle Sook's sound after we finish this sound?" Jane asks.

Roscoe's face is delighted as he nods his head in agreement and finishes the rest of the hot dogs and churros in front of him.

Once they finish the food, they look over to see how Joe and Lianne are doing and if they have reconciled.

"Well that worked fast." Roscoe said.

They both see Lianne and Joe making out and forgetting the world around them. Their moment of bliss is cut short when the gym teacher sees them kissing and blows his whistle to tell them to knock it off. They quickly part and Lianne starts to blush when she realizes Jane and Roscoe have been watching them.

"Guess you too weren't completely done huh?" Jane says.

Lianne walks back over to them while Joe walks back down the bleachers. She notices only wrappers and says "Y'all couldn't wait for me? I still have the munchies."

Roscoe says, "Yea. We saw your munchies."

"Guess Joe's lips weren't enough for you." Jane chimes in.

Lianne starts to push them both and nudge them so they stop teasing her.

Jane says, "So we're going to skip out and have a memorial toke at Uncle Sook's in a few. You can eat there."

Lianne's face starts to smile as she says, "Yea. But Uncle Sook's isn't free."

"Take one for the team Lianne. We need to give him some business so we can keep smoking there." Roscoe says.

"That's all you care about Roscoe."

Roscoe laughs and says, "I'll say it's priority but not everything I care about."

Jane starts to laugh. "Maybe that's why you want to move to a marijuana state huh?"

"Something like that. I understand herb like it's a part of me. So, I need to be in a profession that I'm passionate about."

Jane and Lianne start to laugh as Roscoe goes on about his future dreams. They don't judge but just let him know not to forget about them. Once people start to head out of the gymnasium for bathroom breaks and touring the building for the last time, the gang grabs their stuff and head out towards the back entrance. They make it past the back gate and head to Uncle Sook's, thinking about all of the smoke sessions they had and how this was the first one without Neal. The walk to Uncle Sook's felt a little melancholy since they knew they were missing someone. Neal was always the delight of the group with his sexual innuendos and jokes. He always backed with Roscoe against the girls and got along with Lianne when it came to fashion and boys. Jane and Neal always had a brother relationship since he felt like a family member since he was with Marcus.

They get to Uncle Sook's and see him through the window talking an order from one of the customers. He smiles at them and motions them to walk back to their usual room. They walk back towards the kitchen and sees the beaded room but instead of feeling the excitement of the smoke session they were about to have; a sensation of grief passes through them and they wallow on it as they sit around the table. They stare blankly at the empty hookah and feel remorse for not having Neal here. Jane looks around and sees Lianne and Neal holding back the tears so she decides to reach into her bag to get her phone and posts a picture of Neal on it. She places it on the hookah to make it seem like he's in his spot with us.

Lianne starts to smile as tears fall down from her eyes and Roscoe tries to keep a brave face and relax. Uncle Sook walks through the beads and sees a picture of Neal leaned up against the hookah. His face turns grim as she says hello to everyone and starts to set up the hookah for them. He places menus on the table and quickly leaves to attend to the rest of his restaurant. Jane helps Roscoe with the set up by lifting up the foil and balancing the coals on them. Roscoe quickly sprinkles the fine particles lying at the bottom of the bag and helps Jane places the foil and coal back onto the hookah.

"Who wants the first hit?" Lianne asks.

"I think Jane should take it since it was her idea." Roscoe says.

Jane obliges their request and lifts up the hose from the side of the hookah. She pauses for a moment before inhaling and says, "To Neal."

Q. IMAGINE

Breathing in the smoke and tasting the herb mixed with the blueberry tobacco makes her smile and be grateful for this time with her friends. Lianne will stay in New York but will venture upstate to a private school for business. Roscoe will travel across the country searching for his dream and enjoying the journey to it. Jane will stay here and travel not far from her home to NYU. She enrolled for a dorm her first year but will hopefully move in with Tola after her parents calm down and feel more secure with her growing up and moving on.

She passes her hose to Lianne after taking a few more hits. She tries to force a smile on her face but her eyes how she is feeling something right now.

"What's wrong?" Lianne asks.

Jane tries to smile again but tears fall from her eyes. "I'm just thinking that after the summer, you guys will be gone and everything is going to change."

Lianne rests her hand on Jane and says "That isn't going to change anything. I want you to come visit and you know I'm going to be here for the vacations."

Jane says "I'm not crying out of remorse or fear. I'm crying because this is something that is going to be an amazing experience for all of us. I'm just proud that we made it this far and that we can start our journey away from our parents. Find out who we truly are when there's no one around to fall back on."

Lianne passes the hose to Roscoe as she leans in and hugs Jane tightly.

Jane says, "I just feel sorry that Neal didn't have the opportunity." she says as she starts to cry.

Roscoe looks down to hide the tears falling from his eyes.

"But I know he's in a happy place. And he's happy with my brother so that's okay."

Lianne and Jane start to cry together as Roscoe keeps taking hits from the hookah to hide his emotions. Eventually the two girls wrap up their tears and sorrows to enjoy their last time at Uncle Sook's and enjoy the time together before tomorrow.

CHAPTER XII

Jane wakes up this morning with a shiny smile on her face since it's the day she gets to start her new beginning and work on her dreams. She wakes up earlier than usual to go out with her mom and run errands before meeting at the high school to receive her diploma. Jane showers and then throws on some lounge clothes before meeting her mother downstairs to start their mother-daughter graduation errands. They walk out to the town car and head around New York City to the hair salon, nail salon and Sephora to get her makeup done. They enjoy the morning out together and spending time making Jane out to look like a princess for her graduation.

As they head back home, they smell a beautiful aroma from outside of their house. To their surprise, they see two chefs leaving the house and heading to their cars up the block. Jane and Billie look at each other in surprise until they walk into the house and see an entire spread laid out on the dining room with Isaac standing in the kitchen looking prideful at the image of his wife and daughter. Their faces filled with amazement makes him feel joy inside. Jane's eyes widen at the sight of freshly made corn beef hash, hash browns, and chocolate pancakes.

She sees multiple variations of eggs and French toast. Jane runs to her father and jumps on him to thank him for this spread. Meanwhile Billie trails behind and gives him a warming kiss while Jane grabs the picture of Marcus from the kitchen table.

She places the picture across from her as Billie and Isaac sit at the heads of the table. They stare at each other before digging in and start to enjoy the feast in celebration of Jane's graduation. Jane feels so blessed as she looks at the table doesn't see an inch of it that isn't covered in food. She enjoys the sights of the various dishes of food but immediately dives into the plate of corn beef hash and succulent strawberry filled French toast before Isaac chimes his glass to make a speech.

"This breakfast feast that I orchestrated was dedicated to my loving family and my beautiful daughter and all of her accomplishments this year. This morning is the end of an era for Jane and tomorrow will start a new beginning as a high school graduate and freshman at NYU. Bravo Jane. I'm proud of you. I love you. And I can't wait to see the person you are going to grow up to be."

Jane raises her glass and smiles passionately at her parents.

"Oh. And there's champagne in those glasses. You're an adult now so you get to drink mimosas with us."

Jane smiles before sipping the mimosa and digging into the lovely breakfast on her plate. Billie and Isaac hold hands as they watch their daughter's smile as she bites into the strawberry filled French toast. They have hours before graduation starts so they spend time enjoying breakfast and enjoying each other's company.

After breakfast and their bellies are stuffed with delicious food, Isaac walks into the bedroom to get one more gift for Jane. He walks out of the bedroom with a beautiful black and red dress and presents this to her. Jane jumps in surprise and covers her mouth to hide her grin and blushing cheeks.

"The final gift for my strong daughter. You deserve it girl." he says.

Jane hugs her father tightly, squeezing the dress and him at the same time. Billie watches her happiness from a distance and enjoys every bit of her joy that she shows.

"Your mother helped me pick it out." Isaac says.

Jane runs over to her mom and gives her a warming hug too. Jane walks back to her dad and takes the dress from her in order to get ready to go. She models the dress in front of her mirror as soon as she puts in on and finds a pair of black heels to go with it. Jane stands there proud as she finds the woman in her teenage body. She starts to put on her gown and zipping it in the back. The cap now fits perfectly on her long straight hair. She takes one more glance at herself in the mirror before heading down stairs and showing her parents how she looks in her cap and gown.

After modeling for them and taking pictures, they walk to a town car and head to the school. In front of the school, they see all of the seniors in their cap and gowns walking towards the auditorium for graduation. She sees Lianne and her family along with other students' families and walk to meet up with them. Lianne and Jane smile at each other and try to hug without ruining each other's makeup.

"I can't believe we're doing this!" Jane says with excitement.

Lianne looks around and tries to take in everything that is happening without getting overwhelmed. The seniors are called to the auditorium as the parents start to find seats in the auditorium.

The teachers start to organize them by alphabetical order and prepare them for the walk. Once they are all seated in the auditorium, Jane looks around to see where her parents are and where Lianne and Roscoe are.

The ceremony commences and Jane listens to all the people on the board and principals say their speech about the class and about the future. After a few more speakers, Monica walks on the stage to start her valedictorian speech. She talks about how this school has impacted her life, how the teachers motivate her to pursue her dreams and the friendships she felt from her fellow classmates. After a few moments into her speech she decides to talk about Neal.

"Although this class is filled with such talented individuals. One of us has fallen that should be recognized before we move our tassels and toss our hats into the air. As you may know, our fellow classmate Neal passed away tragically in the beginning of the year. Neal was a bright, charismatic student that everyone knew and loved. Trying to move on from his death was hard on the class entirely and even hard for members of the staff that knew him and loved him. Although Neal is unable to physically walk with us, I hold up an honorary diploma for him to give to his family as a token from the school to honor his life and passing."

She holds up a golden leaf diploma wrapped in red and black ribbon with the school logo on top. She gives it to one of the underclassmen to give to Neal's family after graduation and continues her speech by saying,

"The diploma represents a tribute from the school to honor Neal. Yet from his classmates, one of us who would like to remain anonymous created a beautiful poem in honor of him. The poem is not a memorial to him but an encouragement to us. To never let fear stop you. Never let challenge or change prevent you from moving on. Because strength is always within you and strength always prevails. This poem was written to encourage us to embrace the good and the bad. To know that the good is a blessing and the bad is a lesson to learn. To understand that life is a rollercoaster that has its ups and down but is one hell of a ride. So, keep striving."

Monica begins to read the poem aloud as Jane begins to look around at the reactions of her peers and families in the audience.

> Had hard days and hard nights living this life,
>
> Searching for a reason to sustain and endure this fight.
>
> Running through my mind. In and out. Searching past the doubt,
>
> Gathering my sanity. Getting my plan to test what life's about.
>
> On my path to awakening, dodge the stumbles, people trying to shake me,
>
> People trying to break me with their hating but that mindset didn't phase me.

The only person I can be is the one that strives without admitting defeat,

The one who ventures past the current beliefs and seeks the knowledge of living in sync.

To find that is true,

That happiness was always within you.

To find out that doubt you feel,

Was a defense of the mind and nothing real.

Discover strength is your will,

You have the ability to develop and instill.

The dreams and thoughts you want to produce,

The ideas and beliefs the world needs from you.

Though there may be a time when challenges come and block you on your path,

Forcing you to stare into the hurt, taking your mind off your goals and the means to get past,

But then you'll have a time, a point in your life where you have to survive,

Buckle down and strive. Press the pedal and drive towards happiness in life,

Pushing past the moments you drowned,

Pushing past the times you felt bound,

Drifting past all your fears and concerns,

Those trials that almost left you back and deterred,

Almost took away your happiness and life,

Almost left you in a puddle of strife,

But you splashed through that puddle and found some sweet hope,

Changed your mindset and turned that strife into a

joke.

You stopped and made amends showing what you're all about,

That these demons could never keep you down,

Looking at them as you stand in your glory

Realizing the hurt only gave you an epic story,

You built your strength with the pain, found bliss in disdain.

Kept moving and found the ability to remain.

You battled and made it through that hell,

Finding at the finish line, you worst mistake was doubting yourself.

You were always worthy,

You were always strong,

You always had the opportunity. It was with you all along.

And now that you have found that and started living your dreams,

Proving to yourself that your trials had meaning,

Encourage the next group who lack the esteem,

Lack the motivation to foresee and believe.

Cause you shared in the knowledge of the past. All of those trials and tribulations on your path that you passed,

Because alas, after all that you've seen, you have reached the courage to surpass.

Be free.

There's a moment of silence after Monica finishes to read the poem. Until Neal's family stands up and starts to clap, creating a domino effect with the surrounding audience. Eventually the entire auditorium stands up and applauds Monica for her speech. Monica gives a quick glance at Jane before heading off to the stage as Jane embraces what Monica did for her.

Jane sits in her chair. The only one still sitting after Monica's speech. She sits and takes in what this year has been and who she is in this moment now. After everything she has been through and everything she has overcome. As Jane takes in the applause and the heightened emotion of the day. She hears a familiar voice say.

Well done.

ABOUT THE AUTHOR

Q. Imagine

I began writing poetry at age 11 as an outlet in early adolescence. I fell in love with the freedom of expressing myself through poetry and how my words could be kept to myself if I chose not to share. It was after graduating from college that I started writing the novel Exhale, allowing me to fall in love with creating stories and pursuing a writing career.

BOOKS IN THIS SERIES

The Exhale Chronicles
Experience the life of a young, African American teenager as she grows up within the city streets of New York.

As Jane Mackenzie lets out an Exhale
to find A Soul Spoken
only to Reveal
A Hidden Truth.

A Soul Spoken (2022)

Discover and relive the story of Jane Mackenzie, 3 years after the kidnapping as she attends her junior year of college. Jane has to investigate a cold case for her senior year seminar paper. She winds up stumbling upon one at an subway station when she meets a homeless woman carrying old missing persons fliers. As Jane investigates and dives deeper into the woman's story, she finds chilling similarites between the woman and her kidnapping from 3 years ago. The further Jane investigates, the more she discovers. Until her discovery brings her back to the chaos she had to escape.

Reveal

After discovering and reliving brutal moments from her past, Jane goes on a spiritual quest to find a new life.

A Hidden Truth

To Be Announced

Made in the USA
Middletown, DE
24 September 2025